OLD

HAWK'S

GOLD

OLD HAWK'S GOLD

By
MARY M. DUGGAN

Steck-Vaughn Company
Austin, Texas

To Tim
and Marylu

1 THE REAL GOOD FIND

TIM SCOTT was looking for arrowheads. Tim Scott was always looking for arrowheads . . . and broken pottery, empty birds' nests, rocks, driftwood, even popsicle sticks.

Joe was looking for lizards. Joe was always looking for lizards . . . and lizards, and more lizards.

"That goofy, dumb dog just has a one track mind," Tim snorted to his horse, Skyrocket, as they plunged downhill before a stream of rocks and dirt with Tim digging his heels into his mount's sides. "What good are lizards? If he would dig up a few arrowheads or some Indian pottery, now that would be worthwhile."

Sky lurched up a rise and Tim reined in, looking up. The sun was almost overhead, and Tim was expecting his cousin, Marylu, to drive into the K-I ranch-yard by noon, her father at the wheel and her horse, Blue Girl, following in a trailer. Marylu had wanted a horse for so long, and now she had one. Tim imagined his sense of anticipation was because of Blue Girl.

1

Tim whistled sharply through his fingers for Joe. A bark off to the right answered him. Waiting, Tim took off his hat and rubbed his cropped, sandy hair. Replacing his hat, he whistled again, then saw a little cloud of dust puffing up from behind some boulders beside a small wash, below him and to the right.

"Yeah, that figures," Tim muttered under his breath. "Lizards again!"

He poked Skyrocket to life and down they went to Joe. There was always the chance that Joe might come across something other than lizards.

"Whoop! Whoop! Whoop!" Joe hooted as he scrambled around under the bushes, whipping the branches this way and that. Twigs snapped. Pebbles flew.

Tim jumped down from Sky. Something dark darted among the fallen leaves and twigs. Joe looked up and waited for Tim's praise, his long, red tongue lolling.

"Ah, Joe, it's only a lizard. What do you want to waste your time on those for?"

Joe wrinkled up his forehead and peered at Tim with disappointment, then returned his attention to the fallen leaves, watching for the lizard's next move, while Tim looked about in the sand. Joe certainly hadn't dug up anything interesting.

Tim broke off a switch from a clump of oak brush and whipped at his boots. How could he ever earn any extra money? Sometimes it was tough living

on a ranch. There were no neighbors having lawns
to mow or windows to wash. To save enough out of
his allowance to buy the bicycle he wanted so badly
would take years.

Tim thought about his rock collection, his pieces
of driftwood, and the Indian relics he had found.
Lots of folks seemed to want specimens of these
things. The few nice pieces of driftwood in his collection, and a half dozen perfect arrowheads, surely
wouldn't bring much.

Tim tossed the oak switch away, and stooped to
pick up Sky's reins, but dropped them again. What
had he seen when he tossed the stick across the wash?
Following with his eyes the route the stick had
taken, he located the strangely rounded shadow in
the forking trunk of a big juniper tree. Eyes squinted,
Tim watched the shadow. It didn't move; anyhow,
it was too round to be an animal.

He shuffled through the sand across the wash,
watching cautiously. He grabbed hold of the tree
and pulled himself up. The rounded object was
some kind of pot, Indian work obviously. It was
quite large, being almost a foot across the open top,
and bellying out at the middle.

Tim tried to lift it. It was wedged tight. He
climbed to a branch above, braced himself, and
pulled gently. Finally the pot came free, and Tim
lowered it and himself branch by branch.

He examined his find—earth-brown in color; and

3

when he tapped it with his knuckle, there was a dull, bell sort of sound.

"Man, oh man, this is more like it," Tim said, his excitement mounting. "This must be Indian pottery, all right." He looked inside, and found traces of black running up the sides from a very dark bottom. The pot might have held hot coals at one time, and Tim knew that was one of the ways the Indians had used to bake their pottery.

He carried the big pot across the wash to Skyrocket. "Now hold still," Tim warned Sky with a firm pat on the neck. "This isn't a bedroll I'm carrying." He mounted, pulling himself up with his left hand while holding the pot tightly in his right arm.

"Joe, you old flea hound, I guess you're good enough at picking the right places to look, even if you don't pick the right things to look for." Joe wagged his tail and went on rooting and sniffing.

Tim rode to where he had left his father mending a section of fence. Dutch Scott was just packing his tools away into a canvas sack when Tim came toward him, balancing the pot against Skyrocket's sideways gait down the slope.

"What's that you've got, Son?"

"I found it back there in a juniper. Where do you suppose it came from? It's Indian, isn't it? And why was it up in a tree?"

"Whoa, there, Tim, one at a time!" his father said. "It looks old all right, and it certainly looks

4

Indian, but how it got in a tree, I don't know." As he spoke, Dutch looped the string of the canvas bag around his saddle horn, and mounted his horse. They started off, Tim leading the way with the big pot resting against his thigh, his right arm cradling it carefully.

They came to the edge of the creek that wound past the K-I ranch house. They rode their horses down into the creek bed, stopping to let them drink from a trickle of water. Then they proceeded along the bottom in the direction of the ranch house.

"Do you think it would be worth anything?" Tim asked hopefully, about the pot.

"Don't know," said his Dad. "Years ago, I guess Apaches were pretty thick in through these hills. When I was about your size and had a little more time, I used to pick up arrowheads and pieces of pottery just as you're doing. But I never found anything like your pot there. That's a real good find."

Tim took a big breath and admired his pot. "Boy, wait 'til Marylu sees this," said Tim. "Say, I'll bet she's at the ranch now." Tim dug his heels into Skyrocket's sides, yelling over his shoulder, "I'm going on and see."

"Wait up, Tim, that sand is mighty soft to run Sky in." Dutch's words were wasted, for Tim had shot on ahead.

Rounding a little bend, Skyrocket let out a squeal and leaped quickly to the left. Caught unaware, Tim sailed off, carrying his pot.

The fall into soft sand had not hurt him. He sat up, scolding. "You crazy idiot, Sky, what are you trying to do? Kill me?" Then he saw that the pot had struck a stone outcrop and lay a few feet away . . . just a pile of chips.

"Oh, you dumb horse! Now look what you've done." Tim got to his feet just as Dutch came around the bend. Tim's father pulled up and regarded the remains.

"Well, Tim, you ought to know by now when you run a horse in this loose sand, you take a chance on him stumbling."

"He didn't stumble," Tim objected. "Something spooked him. He shied."

"Yeah?" Dutch cocked one eyebrow and climbed off his horse, shaking his head. He took a piece of canvas out of his saddle bag. "Well, it's too bad. That was a mighty nice pot. Let's wrap up the pieces. Maybe you can glue it back."

Silently, Tim helped his Dad gather the pieces.

"I'll finish here, Son. You go check Sky," Dutch suggested.

Tim walked over to Skyrocket, who stood forlornly on the far side of the creek, his eyes still wide with fright. Tim rubbed his neck, thinking that the sturdy little paint horse was not given to foolish behavior. Sky nuzzled Tim as he pulled at the cinch and wig-wagged the saddle. Nothing seemed out of order. Tim swung up.

He patted Skyrocket on the neck, speaking softly and kindly. "It's all right, Sky. I know you aren't really a dumb, idiot horse." He poked him gently. They started off, Tim glancing back at the shadowy bushes along the other side of the creek.

"I wonder what scared him," he thought to himself. "Something really did!"

2 MARYLU AND BLUE GIRL

MARYLU AND her father, with Blue Girl, had not yet driven onto the flat surrounding the ranch house when Tim arrived there. He unsaddled Sky, brushing the young gelding before turning him into the corral.

He gathered up the makeshift sack that Dutch had filled with pieces of the broken Indian pot and went to his room. He looked around the room. The surface and drawers of his desk were full. The top of his chest of drawers was full. The book shelves were full. Placing the canvas bag on his bed, Tim fetched a card table, which he set up by the window. Untying the canvas, he placed the shards one by one on the table.

"Whew! This is going to be one whopper of a jigsaw puzzle to work," Tim said to himself.

He decided to put all the rim pieces together, and had found ten of these, when outside, an automobile horn sounded faintly.

"It's them!" Tim shouted ungrammatically, and knocked over his chair in his haste. A glance out the window told him that indeed, they had brought Blue Girl, since there was a horse trailer attached to the automobile moving toward the ranch house.

Hastening to leave the house and meet the on-coming car, Tim thought that this would be Mary-lu's first summer at the ranch with her own horse to ride. He knew from her letters how she had saved her allowance and her birthday and Christmas gifts of money; had ironed and done baby sitting; work-ing and saving for a whole year in order to have enough to buy Blue Girl. It must be really tough to own a horse when you didn't live on a ranch where there were scads of them to choose from, Tim thought. He felt he understood what this meant to Marylu because of wanting a bike so much, and not knowing how to earn money to buy one.

As Tim opened the gate of the yard and started across the flat to meet the car and horse trailer, he began to think that it had been a long time since last summer. Maybe Marylu had changed. She was two years older than he was and lived in a town, which was what he thought he wanted; and she could have bought a new bike instead of Blue Girl. Tim walked on slowly and tried to think of what he would say to her.

Marylu had written that Blue Girl was a very special horse, a blue roan. She had written that you just didn't find many blue roans anymore. Tim couldn't remember having ever seen a blue roan horse. Blue Girl must be really something.

He met the pickup just as it came to a stop under a juniper tree on the flat in front of the ranch house yard. Marylu was sitting beside her father, a cowboy hat on her dark, short hair.

"Hi!" said Marylu.

"Hi," said Tim. He kicked a rock, took his hands out of his pockets, and crossed his arms over his chest. "So you brought her, huh?"

Marylu opened the door and got out. "I wouldn't have come without her, would I?" she replied, her brown eyes teasing.

Tim grinned, deciding that Marylu was still Marylu. He walked around and spoke to his Uncle Dave before turning back to Marylu, saying, "Well, let's see her."

Marylu herself opened the half door of the horse trailer and unfastened the leather guard across the opening, talking the whole time.

"Prepare yourself for a big deal. There just isn't another one like her. She's about the smartest, most beautiful horse you'll ever see." At the front of the trailer, she opened a small upper door to unfasten the leather strap which held Blue Girl's head in place while she was in the trailer stall.

"Okay, Blue Gee, come on out," Marylu said, lightly slapping the animal's shoulder. Blue Girl shifted her feet and backed out of the trailer. She put her head down to the ground and sniffed.

"Well," said Marylu, "what do you think? Isn't she something?"

10

Tim wiped his sleeve across his mouth. So this was Blue Girl. She looked just like any other old black horse to him. What was so special? The way she was standing, she certainly didn't look as if she were such a big deal. She just looked kind of saggy and droopy and dirty black.

"Well?" Marylu repeated, stroking Blue Girl with pride, and imagining Tim as truly impressed.

"Oh, she's all right; yes, sir, she's all right." Tim was working to put some excitement in the words. "Yeah, she's really okay. How old is she; do you know?"

"Well, actually, she's about ten, or maybe twelve years old. But she's still got lots of pep, and the man we bought her from said he thought she had some thoroughbred in her on account of how her head looks."

"You mean the way it's kind of long for the rest of her?" Tim asked, aware that twelve was really quite old for a horse.

Marylu eyed him and asked, "What do you mean by that?"

"It's real nice that way," Tim said quickly. "It gives her a . . . well, sort of a distinguished look." Tim guessed he'd better start being very careful what he had to say about Blue Girl.

"Um, that's what I thought too," Marylu said, satisfied. She led Blue Girl over to the water trough by the barn, and the mare drank gratefully. Marylu splashed some water on her and rubbed her.

"That's a long, hot old trip for a horse, you know," she remarked over her shoulder to Tim. "There, do you see the white hair in her coat?"

Tim moved closer and looked. Sure enough she wasn't exactly a black horse at all, but salted with thousands of white hairs.

"That's why she's a blue roan," Marylu explained. "Sometimes when the light is at just the right angle, she looks like a blue horse because of the highlights from the white hair showing through. Then she really is beautiful."

"Yeah?" Tim said, trying to please.

"But now she's tired and dusty from the trip."

"Oh, sure," Tim said.

"Where shall I put her?"

Tim walked to the corral gate. "Bring her over here. She might as well get acquainted now with Sky."

They turned Blue Girl into the corral and followed Dutch and Uncle Dave into the house. Tim and Marylu fixed a pitcher of ice water, while Tim's parents, Uncle Dave, and Grandpa Cone caught up on the news since the last letters had been exchanged. Tim and Marylu had their own conversation. He told her about the pot he had found, and what had happened to it.

As they started toward Tim's room to inspect the shards, Tim overheard his father telling Uncle Dave that representatives of a mining company had visited the ranch, asking to look around for possible sites for test drilling.

"Do they think there's copper on the ranch?" Uncle Dave asked.

"Oh, I don't think so," Tim's father said. "As I understand it, drilling at one place can be helpful toward locating minerals of any kind in the area anywhere. They could have chosen a neighboring ranch or even government land." Glancing back, Tim saw his father scratching his ear, a sign of indecision in Dutch. "I guess I can't refuse. The company has promised to put in a few roads, and that will certainly be a big help out here in these rocks. But I will hate the traffic going through."

Tim said to Marylu, "Hey, maybe something exciting will happen around here for a change . . . them drilling holes and going back and forth with rigs, and things."

"Something exciting?" asked Marylu. "What's exciting about drilling holes?" Tim knew that she would gladly trade places with him, just to live on a ranch. She didn't know how tiresome it could be, particularly when there was no one to plan things with.

"This is what's left of the pot I found," Tim said.

Marylu stared at the hodge-podge on the card table in front of her. "Oh, Tim, how do you expect to fix a mess like that?"

Tim said quietly, "It was the best thing I ever found. I thought maybe it might be worth something. You see, I want to do the same as you did. I want to earn money to buy something I want. And there's just not much way to get money on a ranch."

Marylu looked sympathetic. "I hadn't realized. I guess it really would be hard to earn money out here. What is it you want so much?"

Tim paused. He seemed to know how she was going to respond. Then he said boldly, "It's a bicycle."

Marylu hooted. "But *anybody* can have a bicycle!"

"Well, *I* can't," Tim said. "For two years, every Christmas and birthday, I've asked for a bike. Mom and Dad just say I've got a horse for any riding I want to do; and if I really want a bike, I'll have to spend my own money for it."

"But why do you want a bike? With the ranch, and Joe, and the horses . . . ?"

"Didn't *you* want a bicycle?" Tim asked. "And didn't you get one when you were even younger than me?"

"Well, sure," Marylu admitted. "But what I really wanted was a horse."

"Try to see that getting a bicycle is just as big a thing to me as getting Blue Girl was to you."

Marylu turned her brown gaze on Tim, saying silently, "I understand. I will help you." What she said aloud was, "Where will you ride your bike?"

"There's plenty of room on the flat," Tim said. "I don't care that it isn't paved. I just want one. I can have one when I can buy it myself, but to save enough out of my allowance would take forever."

"And you think this pot might be worth money?" Marylu looked doubtfully at the broken bits on the table.

"Well—I don't know. It was such a big pot, and it might be a hundred years old. There might be someone who would want to give me something for it."

Marylu sighed, "Tomorrow, we'll start on it, but I think you're crazy to want a bike."

"Yeah," said Tim. "Crazy like you wanting Blue Girl."

They grinned at each other. Marylu wondered why Tim couldn't see the difference between a living animal and a collection of pedals and brakes. Tim was thinking, "When I get my bike, it sure won't be twelve years old!" If they didn't quite understand each other, at least their friendship was real.

3 THE SPOOKER

NEXT MORNING, the plans were to start gluing the shattered pot immediately after a short workout with the horses. Uncle Dave stayed around long enough to see his daughter and Tim saddle up. He kissed Marylu goodbye, shook hands with Tim, and drove off, waving farewells to Mom and Dutch on the porch, and to the young riders preparing to mount.

"Well, let's see what she can do," Tim said.

Marylu headed Blue Girl across the flat. Either the mare was cautious in her new surroundings, or, as Tim suspected, she was much slower-gaited than Sky. He was intrigued at noticing that Marylu seldom used the reins. Her movements in the saddle appeared to be sufficient to direct Blue Girl.

Tim gave Sky a kick and joined Marylu. Together, they put the horses through their paces. When it was over, Tim had to admit to himself that Blue Girl had worked out better than he had imagined she would.

16

After the horses had been put up, the pair went to Tim's room, where the shards lay just as they had left them yesterday when Marylu had first viewed the sad mess.

"I've got it figured out this way," Tim said. "If we get all the rim pieces together, then the flatter bottom pieces together, the curved part ought to be a snap."

Marylu fitted a pillow from Tim's bed into her chair at the card table, curling one leg under her as she sat down.

"Um-hum, it'll probably be a snap all right," she said. "Before we're through with this mess, I'll be snapping at you, and you'll be snapping at me." They began sorting pieces into groups. "You wrote me about finding arrowheads in some ruins. Tell me more about it."

Tim ceased working. "We call the place Rose Hill. First I noticed rocks stacked up that looked like walls of rooms, and then I found potsherds or shards, that's what archaeologists call pieces of broken pottery. One place must have been where they made their fires. It was full of potsherds and stuff, and lots of charcoal all through the dirt. I've been digging around there ever since."

"Have you found anything else?" Speaking, Marylu kept turning the burned pieces so that the black streaks were exposed.

"The arrowheads were the best things so far," Tim replied, "but I know somebody lived there, and I think something good is bound to turn up sooner or later. I pack some tools up there every now and then, but it's real hard digging."

"Is it far away?" asked Marylu.

"A mile or so, I guess. I'll take you up there one day soon."

Marylu scooted her chair back, saying, "We need some glue."

"I'll get it," Tim said.

"Oh, no you don't!" Marylu pushed him back in his chair. "You tell me where it is, and I'll get it, while you do some work for a change."

"Okay, okay! The glue ought to be on the bookshelves where my airplane models are." Tim resumed the work of sorting while Marylu got the glue.

She had barely returned to the card table when Tim reached for the glue, saying, "Here's two that fit."

Marylu sighed. "You would find the first pieces, after I did all the work of turning them so you could see the black streaks."

"Yeah, that really helps. Say, this glue isn't going to work very good. See how they fall apart."

"Oh, you stupe!" Marylu laughed. "Don't you know with pottery you have to let the glue dry on each piece the first time?"

He watched while she worked with the pieces, her fingers slender and deft.

She explained. "If you keep the glue thin enough the second time, it goes together smooth, with no

18

gobs sticking out." She held the two pieces together and waited for them to set. "We're going to need masking tape to hold them until they're dry; otherwise, this will take forever. I think I have some with my paint things in my traveling case."

"I'll get it," Tim offered, starting up again.

"Never mind," said Marylu. "I'll do the getting. You do some work."

"Hey, hey! What's all this about?" said Grandpa Cone from the doorway.

"Hi, Grandpa," said Tim, beckoning him in.

"What are you two doing?" asked Grandpa.

"We're trying to put this pot together that Tim had to go and break," explained Marylu.

"Say, Grandpa, why don't you help us? It's lots of fun, just like working a jigsaw puzzle," Tim said hopefully.

Grandpa looked at their upturned faces, then said, "Well, I guess I can try."

While Tim fetched another chair, Marylu got the masking tape. Soon they were all settled around the table.

"You know, Tim, when I was a youngster, I used to hunt for Apache tears," Grandpa Cone said.

"I didn't know the Apaches ever cried. I thought they were real tough," Marylu said.

"Are you trying to be funny?" Tim asked severely.

"Probably Marylu has never heard about Apache Leap," Grandpa said. "It all happened right here, almost in the back yard."

Grandpa fitted two pieces together, and looked about for a third. "Back in the seventies," he went on, "somebody discovered silver over near Globe. Then the white folks moved in on the land that the government had agreed to give the Apaches for their own. It started off a war that lasted many years, and on both sides, many lives were lost. About four hundred cavalrymen were garrisoned right down the road there at the Pinal Ranch."

"That's quite a way from town," Tim commented.

"That's right, Tim, but supplies had to come through these mountains. Those soldiers had a certain job to do. It was Camp Pinal then. Soldiers were sent out from the camp to stations on top of some of the rocky pinnacles around here, where they could keep track of the Indians moving all about the area. When they saw anything amiss, they would signal the camp with mirrors."

"Here, you Indian trackers, maybe some lemonade would help you track those pieces faster." Tim's Mom scooted three icy glasses into the clutter on the table. "It seems to me," she added, surveying the room, "that with this Indian pot scattered about, and your collection of rocks, old bird nests, driftwood specimens and other odds and ends, you'll barely have a path left to your bed."

"Ah, there's lots of room left. Take a look under my bed," Tim suggested.

"Thank you, no. I can see enough jungle creeping in from here, and if you don't get that pot pasted together quickly, I'm afraid the whole room will be lost to human sight forever. Please, keep at the job. I'll bring more refreshment whenever you weaken."

Tim set his glass down and began working. "Go on, Grandpa, tell us about Apache Leap." He had heard the story often without ever growing bored by it. Marylu would be hearing it for the first time.

"Well, one day a signal operator, who had been watching the retreat of an Apache raiding party, discovered this long-searched-for hideaway the Indians had used as home base. The cavalry from Camp Pinal was sent after them. Hand me that little black piece there, Tim."

Tim pushed it across the table, saying, "What happened then, Grandpa?"

"Well, the Indians were about seventy-five, and almost the whole four hundred cavalrymen were hot behind them. The cavalrymen drove them to the very top of the cliff above their hideaway. It looked like a sure surrender. But just as the four hundred reached the top of the cliff, all the Apaches jumped off the edge to their deaths on the rocks below."

"Good grief!" said Marylu. "Is that cliff around here?"

Tim answered her. "Apache Leap is that big, red cliff left of the highway, after you go through the tunnel towards Superior. You've seen it lots of times."

"And that's where the tears come in," Grandpa

said. "They say all the squaws of those Indians came to that spot beneath the cliff and wept for their braves, and that their tears turned to glass. You can find them all about nearby. Here's one on my key chain. See, it is smokey-colored, and shaped rather like a tear drop."

Marylu looked at the bit of glass. "It's pretty," she said, quietly moved by the story.

"Geologists call these obsidian, and say they are formed by volcanoes, but I don't think that's nearly as good a story," concluded Grandpa.

"Do you suppose there would be any Indian bones left around there?" Tim asked.

"From their jump, you mean?"

"Oh, Tim, what a horrible thought." Marylu closed her eyes.

"Say, you're not working very hard," Grandpa remarked to Tim, who began again trying to fit pieces together.

"There used to be an old Indian," Grandpa said, "who lived up in the hills. He was tall with hawklike eyes, and he walked so quietly that he gave folks quite a jolt. Old Hawk claimed that his father was one of the braves that went over Apache Leap. Now where did that tape go?"

"Here it is," Marylu said. "Did he hold it against the white people because of Apache Leap?"

"I don't think so, Marylu. But I expect he got a certain pleasure out of shaking them up the way he did. He didn't have any family and he always stayed to himself, camping here and there among the hills, probably in caves. No one ever knew him to work, but he was always provided for. In dry years, or when things were extra tough for him, he would appear at a store in one of the towns nearby, asking to trade against a gold nugget."

Tim's eyes opened wide. "A gold nugget!"

"Yep," continued Grandpa, "he would trade it for provisions and have money left over for months. Lots of Apaches used to trade that way, but only when they really needed something. No one ever knew where they got the nuggets. And they surely never told."

"Maybe he found them around here!" Struck by this idea, Tim stopped working.

"I wouldn't know. Old Hawk was finally killed by careless hunters in the thirties. Folks kind of missed his swooping down on them the way he had done. Somehow a story got started that every time a horse got 'scary,' it was really Old Hawk's ghost sneaking up just as he always had done. Well, well, this pot of yours is beginning to take shape, Tim."

"Grandpa, do you think that old Indian could be a ghost running around?" Tim asked.

"Heh, heh, well, Tim, it's hard to say. Some folks can imagine a lot of things."

"Maybe it was the ghost that spooked Sky yesterday."

"Tim! Marylu! Where are you?" It was Dutch, calling from out in the flat.

"Are you birds going to leave me with all the work?" Grandpa called after them.

"We'll be back," Marylu promised.

Tim and Marylu ran across the flat to where Dutch was unsaddling his horse. Jennie, the mule, was standing nearby with something brownish and furry draped across her back.

"Gee, Dad, what is it?" Tim asked.

"A mountain lion, Tim. I killed it very near the spot where Sky tossed you in the sand yesterday. I guess this is the 'spooker.' "

Tim thought about what Grandpa had said about Old Hawk's ghost. He looked at the lion, and thought that if Old Hawk's ghost had ever been near, it had probably been frightened away by this big cat.

"What are you going to do with him, Uncle Dutch?" Marylu asked.

"I'm going to load him in the pickup and take him into town. There's a bounty on those 'calf eaters'—seventy-five dollars."

"Wow!" thought Tim. "Seventy-five dollars! Money like that could buy one very fine bike."

4 SETTING TRAPS

EARLY NEXT morning, Tim and Marylu were out in the old shed by the house, a shed Mom had threatened to have torn down. Tim had just finished unloading a big wooden barrel into a trunk with no lid.

"It's not there," he reported. Choosing next a tall Mexican basket, he began to unload its contents into the barrel he had just emptied.

"If I knew what a coyote trap looked like, I'd be more useful," Marylu volunteered.

"Yeah, well," Tim said, smug in his own knowledge, "it's a little hard to explain to a girl."

He tossed an old inner tube into the barrel, then a couple of paint brushes, a strip of screen wire, a pulley wheel, a caulking gun; thus exposing a strong chain, its links rusted. When he saw the big double-pronged hook, he knew he had found the trap. "Here it is!" he shouted.

"Here is what?" Dutch asked from the doorway. "Oh, you two turning trapper?"

"I thought if I got a coyote with this, you'd let me use your big trap for mountain lion, so I could earn seventy-five dollars, like you did," Tim explained.

"It seems in good shape," Dutch said, after checking over the trap. "Are you sure you've found coyote tracks in a good place to trap?"

Tim nodded. "There's a fence on one side, and boulders and brush on the other. He has to go over my trap or else jump the fence."

Dutch said sternly, "You understand that you're taking the responsibility to do this right?"

"Yes, sir, I'll be careful," Tim promised.

While Tim was putting the trap into a canvas bag along with the other things he would need, Marylu went into the house and made two peanut butter sandwiches. She joined Tim at the corral with the sandwiches wrapped in bread paper, and a filled canteen.

When they had saddled their horses, Marylu looped the strap of the canteen over her saddle horn, and Tim tied the canvas bag to one of his saddle-strings. Marylu climbed on Blue Girl and followed Tim across the flat to the oak brush and manzanita beyond the house.

Marylu was pleased and excited over the ride in such wild, beautiful country. This was certainly better than riding at home, on the same old trail just outside of the city.

Tim's dog, Joe, saw the departure. He shook himself, then ducked under the rail fence of the yard, and fell in behind them.

In and out among the brush clumps and trees, over rocks, or around larger rocks, they picked their way, steadily climbing to high ground. They came to a fence and followed along it for about a mile.

"Okay, this is as far as we ride." Tim tied their horses to the fence. With the canvas bag slung over his shoulder, he started out, Marylu following with the canteen.

They walked over a small knoll covered with rusty-red rocks. The rocks became boulders, and, finally, just beyond a very large boulder, Tim stopped before a little pocket of sand. Faint tracks were still there, causing Tim to whistle with satisfaction.

Marylu looked at the chosen place, then at the rugged hills. What a lonely spot. She felt a sudden compunction at the idea of a living creature left to die in a trap.

Joe charged after a scampering lizard. "That dog," Tim said, with affectionate disgust.

After lifting the sandwiches out of the canvas bag, Tim dumped its other contents onto the ground. "Now I'll show you how this is done," he said to Marylu.

"Give me those," she said, and put the sandwiches back into the bag, which she hung from a barb on the fence, away from ants.

Tim scooped out a shallow place in the sand, placing there the big double hook, and on top of that, carefully coiled, the chain. At the end of the chain was the trap, and this he arranged firmly on top of the chain.

Now he slipped a pair of giant wooden pliers over the spring on one side. By doing this, he was able to pull the jaws of the trap apart with his hands until they stayed apart, enabling him to reach beneath and cautiously set the trap. He released the spring with the wooden pliers.

"From here on it's HANDS OFF," Tim said. Marylu watched as he picked from his supplies a piece of cloth. Slowly, using sticks for fingers, he threaded the cloth under one jaw, over the trigger of the trap, and under the other jaw. Then he sprinkled sand lightly over the whole thing.

"You see," he explained, "the cloth keeps the sand, which hides the trap, out of the working mechanism, so it will be ready to snap when Old Man Coyote comes along here." Four tiny twigs stuck in the sand formed a rectangle around the outer edges of the trap. "That's to mark the location of the trap, so we can find it later without getting caught ourselves, in case Old Man Coyote decides not to come this way again."

Tim cleared away a clump of dry grass from between the rocks, and smoothed the sand around the trap, making it look, he hoped, like an inviting pathway. He wiped his hand across his forehead, noticing that it was beginning to get hot. He looked at the sky.

"It's almost noon," he said. "Boy, am I hungry!"

"Can I help you finish whatever else you have to do, so that we can eat our sandwiches?"

Tim considered the offer. "Well, I guess you can help. We'll need to put a barricade around the trap so none of the cattle can get into it."

"Won't it keep the coyote out too?" Marylu asked.

He shook his head. "Coyotes travel in places where cattle can't go. First we need some good strong sticks. I ought to find some up there," and he pointed to a clump of junipers on a rise above.

Carrying his hatchet, he climbed the hill, and chopped off two suitable branches, which he cleaned of small twigs before returning to Marylu. At the corners of the sand pocket, he stuck the branches in the ground and braced them solidly with rocks at the base, leaving them crossing towards each other.

"Now you see how to do it," Tim said. "I'll chop more branches and throw them down to you. You can fix them around this pocket. We'll need a bunch more."

He climbed the hill again. He trimmed another good stick and tossed it down to Marylu. She began setting it in place. Tim pulled at another branch but it caught on the underbrush. When he stooped to free it, he saw a stone different from the others. He threw down his hatchet and dropped to the ground to examine his find.

"Hey, Marylu, come here quick," Tim shouted.

"Why?" Spurred by the excitement in his voice,

29

Marylu started running up the hill. "What is it?"

"Look what I've found!"

"Well, what?" Marylu dropped to the ground beside him.

"It's a metate!" He tugged at it, and moved it a fraction. He struggled some more and slowly pulled it out. Into the hole remaining, a round stone rolled. Tim saw it.

"Wow, and the mano too!" he shouted. He fitted the smaller stone into the hollow of the larger one, demonstrating to Marylu how Indians ground corn.

"The hollow is real deep," she noticed aloud.

"Yeah," marveled Tim. "I wonder how many ears of corn it took to hollow it down that far?"

"Maybe it has never been touched since the Indians used it," Marylu said.

"This is really something! Let's get it home."

"But we haven't finished the barricade, Tim," objected Marylu.

Tim glanced down at the three sticks in the sand pocket. "Ah, it's good enough," he said. "Boy, this metate is heavy!"

"You said yourself we needed more branches."

"The cattle are all down at the other end. Probably they won't be up this way for days. Come on." Tim buttoned the mano safely inside his shirt, and turned to go.

"Bring that branch I cut, and my hatchet," he told Marylu.

She obeyed him, imagining that he meant to add

the branch to the barricade. With great care, Tim rolled the metate stone down the hill. He unhooked the canvas bag from the fence, and started to push the big metate into it.

"What are you trying to do?" asked Marylu. "That fat thing will never go through that opening."

"I think it will if I keep working at it," said Tim. "I don't know how else we can carry it down the trail to the horses. It's mighty heavy, you know."

Tim pulled and tugged at the bag until finally it swallowed the metate stone. He forced the big stone down to the bottom of the bag, folding the open end and wadding it into the hollow of the metate.

"Now give me that branch," said Tim. "And get the strap off of the canteen." He put the branch in the groove of the metate, and when Marylu handed him the strap, he bound the metate firmly to the middle of the sturdy branch.

"But what about the canteen?" asked Marylu. Tim slipped the end of the strap through one bracket of the canteen and fastened the buckle of the strap. Now the canteen was fastened securely with the metate to the middle of the branch.

"Take the other end and let's see if we can carry it," Tim said.

Slowly they lifted the stick with its burdens and made their way with it down the trail, to the horses.

When they reached the horses, they lifted the heavy sack onto Tim's saddle, and Marylu balanced it while Tim crawled on behind. After Tim had adjusted himself to his position behind the saddle, they started back to the ranch.

Grandpa Cone came out when Tim called from the back gate of the house.

"Grandpa, would you take this down for me, please?"

"Great day, Boy," Grandpa said, lifting the heavy sack to the ground, "this doesn't feel like a coyote in here. You must have got a bear."

"No, sir, Grandpa. This is a metate I found. You know, what the Indians used to grind corn. It's just like the pictures I've seen."

With Grandpa's help, Tim shook the big metate free of the sack. Out plopped two peanut butter sandwiches thoroughly flattened. Gravely, Tim handed one to Marylu. The other, he peeled of bread paper, and ate hungrily. After a moment, she followed his example. The sandwiches tasted better than they looked.

Grandpa was saying, "It's a beaut! Did you think to look for the mano stone?"

"It's here, in my shirt."

"You have a good eye, Tim," his grandfather said approvingly.

Tim planned to keep the metate stone in his room. His mother had different ideas. "Now that thing has been outside for heaven knows how long, and it won't hurt it to stay outside a while longer. It's nice, Tim, but just leave it out here."

"I think maybe we better set it down in the shed while you're deciding what to do with it, Tim," Grandpa said.

"Ah, all right," said Tim, "but you'd think somebody would get a little excited about something like this."

"Now, Tim, your Mom thinks highly of all the things you've found, but you'll have to admit your room is beginning to be quite a mess, with all those relics and things. When you decide what you want to do with it, let me know. I'll help you." Grandpa went back into the house.

Tim slumped down in the doorway of the shed. He picked up a stick and scratched in the dirt. He snorted and whipped his boot with the stick.

"Boy," said Tim. "Things are getting mighty bad when you can't even put things in your own room. Here I find something that's probably really worth something, and nobody even cares."

Grandpa was talking to Mom in the kitchen, and his voice carried through the open back door.

"Dutch tells me the mining men are coming tomorrow to make arrangements about the drilling."

"Yes," Mom answered, "I suppose the dust will fly now with all of them going back and forth."

Marylu was trying to change Tim's mood when she suggested, "Why don't we make the shed into a place for your things?"

"This dump? It's already full of stuff, and Mom wants it torn down, too."

"If we cleaned it out and fixed it up, maybe she wouldn't want to have it torn down. It could be a sort of showroom for all the things you've found."

"We can't just throw away the stuff that's in here."

"Some of it we can," said Marylu, "and the rest we can hang on the walls. Those things can be relics of a later date! We can make displays just as they do at the State Museum at home. Maybe we could paint the shed."

Tim examined the shed with new interest. Its two doors could be "IN" and "OUT" doors, he decided. "I could charge admission, and earn money to get my bike," he said.

"Where would you find the people to come?" Marylu asked. She was too fond of Tim to laugh openly at his idea. But a paying museum!—out here!

"I could put a sign down on the highway."

"Would your Dad like that?"

"No, he wouldn't." Then Tim remembered the conversation he had just overheard. "The mining men would come, maybe."

"Not if you try to charge them admission. The shed is still a good place to put your things."

"Okay, where do we start?"

They worked in the shed until Mom called them to wash up for supper. She gave Tim a pan of food for Joe, but although Tim whistled and called for some time, Joe did not come.

"Ah, that crazy dog," Tim said, putting Joe's pan in the usual place. "If he wants to let the cats get his food, it's his tough luck." Tim went into the house, intent on his own supper.

5 THE BOOMERANG

Tim wakened with a plan for getting the mining men to pay to see his relics. He breakfasted early with Dutch, who was to meet with some of the men to discuss the roads they had agreed to build on the ranch.

Although Tim itched to tell about his plan, he seemed not to want to tell his father.

After Dutch left, Tim made as much noise as possible in the living room, which was next to Marylu's bedroom. When she did not come out, he decided to begin without her.

He found two boards just the right size, a brush, and a can of red paint. He took these to the shed, where he began tracing letters on one of the boards.

He had finished the first board and had started on the second before he heard Marylu talking to Mom in the kitchen.

"Hey, Marylu, come on out," Tim called, for he had decided not to bother Mom with this scheme either.

"I'm helping your Mom with the dishes," Marylu called back.

He waited impatiently, listening to their conversation.

Marylu was saying, "Sometime when someone is going to town to shop or something, maybe I could go along to Jane's house, and at least say 'hi' to her."

"Of course, you may," Mom replied. "Since her family had to move, isn't it lucky they managed to move in this direction. At least you will get to see her during the summertime. Why don't you phone her and see when she would like for you to come?"

"Ah, Marylu, come on!" shouted Tim.

"Okay, okay!" She hung the dish towel on the drying rack on the service porch. "You know, I just might have some things of my own to do sometimes," she said as she entered the shed. "What's up?"

"Look," said Tim, and he pointed to the drying boards.

"W-R-E-L-I-C-S! What does that spell?"

"Relics, you know, relics."

"It's spelled R-E-L-I-C-S. It doesn't have a W in front."

"I know that, but don't you get it? The W goes with the W in West. Wrelics of the West. That's the way they do in advertisements. It catches the eye or something."

"Oh. But everyone will think you just can't spell."

The other sign read, ADMISSION $1.00.

"Tim, it's stupid to think you can get anyone to pay a dollar to come in here," Marylu said.

"No, I got it all figured out." She seemed on the point of leaving, so Tim quickly began trying to explain his idea.

He picked up the WRELICS OF THE WEST sign. "This one goes outside where the mining men will see it." He put it down. "But this one doesn't go outside; oh no! This is the one that gets them." He picked up the ADMISSION $1.00 sign, and walked with it to the far door of the shed. "It goes right here on the inside of this door. Just before they leave, and after they have seen everything, I'll be waiting right here to collect the dollar. So what's so stupid about that?"

Marylu's mouth was set in a straight line. "You're right. It's not stupid. It's downright dishonest!"

Tim raised his eyebrows. "What's dishonest about it?" he demanded. "Who says where the admission sign has to be?"

"You know it isn't fair! Probably the men will come in just to be nice to us, and then find they've been tricked. No, I won't have any more to do with it if you're going to do this." Marylu glared at Tim. How could he want to do such a sneaky thing? She went out, saying over her shoulder, "I am going to paint a watercolor."

Tim studied his signs. "Girls are dopes," he said out loud. "They just don't have any business sense."

He heard his father calling him across the yard

fence. Tim poked his head out of the shed. "Yeah, Dad?"

"Where did you set your trap?"

With the signs still in his hands, Tim had to think a minute about which trap Dutch meant. Then he remembered. "Oh, it's up there in the rocks by the fence next to the Meyers place. Why?"

"Something must be in it. There's sure a lot of howling going on up that way. I'm going to take a look."

Tim tossed the signs down. "I'll get Sky and be right with you!" He ran off to the corral.

"Did it sound like a coyote, Dad?" Tim asked, when he had caught up with Dutch.

"I never heard a coyote sound like this did." They trotted along, slowing down only for the rocky places. Finally they reached the fence. Tim headed to the right.

"How far down, Tim?"

"About a mile, I guess."

Suddenly a long, mournful howl rolled down across the rocks. It seemed to make the few thin bushes quiver with its agony, then faded into nothing.

"Gosh, Dad, what was that?"

"Sounds real weird, doesn't it?"

Intermittently as they rode, there was howling; as they came nearer, there were snarling and whimpering sounds.

"Here's where I tied Sky, Dad."

They dismounted. Tim waited for Dutch to get his rifle. They started over the knoll. The rocks became boulders and finally the one large boulder appeared. The howling, moaning cries hurt Tim's ears and made the skin on his back feel creepy.

"I hear something thrashing around, Dad."

Dutch leading, they rounded the big boulder and looked down into the sand pocket. Tim gagged.

"Oh, golly! Oh . . . oh . . . golly! It's Joe!" He started running toward a raging heap of black fur which was crouched in the rocks beyond the sand.

"Tim! Stop!" Dutch yelled. "Don't get too near!"

Tim had dropped to his knees in the sand. "It's all right, Joe. Don't worry now, please, Joe, don't worry. It's all right. We'll get you out, and it'll be all right," Tim pleaded softly.

When Dutch moved toward them, Joe began to throw himself about. He was snarling, and his eyes were wild with fright.

"I'll have to hold him, Tim, while you open the trap."

Dutch watched for an opportunity to grab the crazed dog. Tim, looking about for something to release the spring, saw the wooden pliers. In his haste yesterday to get the metate home, he had forgotten them. He snatched them up.

"Okay, Dad, I'm ready!"

Dutch lunged at Joe, seizing him around the neck with one hand, the other vising his muzzle. The man's legs were locked around Joe's hind quarters.

Tim leaped to the task of releasing the spring and opening the jaws of the trap, slick with Joe's blood.

In spite of all Dutch could do, Joe's struggles kept the trap scooting and bouncing away from Tim's grasp with the pliers.

"Hurry up, Tim, for heaven's sake. I can't hold him all day!"

Tim took a deep breath and thrust the pliers, handles first, at the spring. They slipped over. He threw himself at the handles with all his weight, grabbed the jaws, and pulled. They parted. Joe's paw came out. Dutch let go, and Joe bounded away three-legged into the sand, where he crumpled down, whimpering and licking his paw.

Dutch stood up and looked about. He saw the three juniper branches that Tim and Marylu had left as a barricade.

"What are these for, Tim? And where is the barricade you left for the stock?"

Tim stared at him miserably.

Dutch spoke in reasonable tones. "Tim, a good rancher doesn't trap predators for the bounty. He traps them to keep his stock safe. A good rancher doesn't do a job halfway. He keeps plugging, and follows through to the end. A good rancher takes care of his stock as well as his dog. I have worked hard to make this ranch what it is—"

"I'm sorry, Dad!"

"I know it, Son. That you trapped your dog was not really your fault. Anywhere a coyote can go,

Joe can go too. But you could have trapped a cow—"

"It's Joe I care about," Tim said, fighting not to cry.

"—or a horse. Now Tim, think it over. Because it just isn't good judgment to go after something you want, without thinking about what you might be hurting or destroying on your way." Dutch picked up the trap and his rifle, and started back toward the horses.

Joe had stopped licking his paw. He watched Tim with his big, sad eyes. Tim started crawling toward him, but Joe pulled himself up on three legs and hobbled after Dutch.

Feeling justly abandoned by everyone, Tim started down the trail, carrying the pliers which yesterday he had forgotten.

With Marylu watching, Joe was eating hungrily from his pan near the back door when Tim reached the ranch house. "Do you think his leg is broken?" Tim asked her.

"I don't know, Tim. He won't let me near him."

Tim went into the shed. After awhile, Marylu followed. "While you were gone, Grandpa finished the pot," she said.

"Yeah?" he said, more to be polite than from any real interest.

"I painted a picture while he did it."

"Yeah, I know, you said you were going to."

"Well, look at it."

Tim raised his eyes to the picture Marylu held.

"Hey," he exclaimed, "it's the pot!"

"Like it?"

"It looks just like before I broke it!"

"We can write a letter to the State Museum, sending this picture. They could tell you if the pot is valuable. If it is, you could sell it for bike money."

"I sure won't get to set any traps for awhile, and right now, I don't much want to," Tim confessed.

"I guess you wouldn't," Marylu said. She felt sorry for Tim. She knew how much he cared about Joe in spite of all his rough talk to him. "Maybe the pot will be worth as much as a mountain lion," she said encouragingly.

"Honest?" He looked at her so hopefully, she wished she could tell him exactly what he wanted to hear.

"I don't know, that's for sure. So, come on; let's write that letter and get it in the mail."

6 THE INTRUDERS

THE PAINTED signs Marylu had objected to, Tim put away for safekeeping. If the mended pot were going to prove valuable, he would not need the miners' money to buy his bike. Meanwhile, the idea was a good one of cleaning out the shed to have a place to keep his things.

Tim had unloaded two wheelbarrow loads of rubbish into the garbage pit when Marylu came to find him. When she didn't see the signs, she guessed that Tim had changed his mind about them. She pitched in to help him.

"Let's clean out this old trunk, and then we'll have a place to put things that we want to keep," Marylu suggested.

"Okay," said Tim, and the two of them dug into the undertaking with great energy.

By lunchtime, they were beginning to slow down a bit, and after lunch, they decided they had had enough shed-cleaning for one day.

"I know what we can do," said Tim. "Let's saddle up, and I'll take you to Rose Hill where my diggings are. Maybe we'll run across some more arrowheads or something."

"Oh neat!" cheered Marylu. "I've never found an arrowhead."

They were soon on their way to Rose Hill, glad to be out of the dust and hodge-podge in the old shed. Crossing the creek, they followed along its edge for a mile or so. They cut up through the manzanita, away from the creek, following a well-used path in and out through the rocks and brush.

"No wonder it's called Rose Hill," Marylu said. "The rocks are really red. Even the soil is red, and it's pretty."

"That shows there's mineral in the soil," explained Tim. "When air hits the iron, it always does that. Lots of the hills for miles around here have that red color. And there's lots of mining done in them too, silver and gold as well as copper. But I guess the Indians liked Rose Hill because it was a good spot to hide in among these rocks, high enough to see around, and with water in the creek right below."

"How many Indians were here, do you know?" asked Marylu.

"Oh, I think this had been sort of a permanent camp for a long time. Some of them may have stayed for considerable periods. Anyway, I've spotted outlines of at least eight or ten dwelling places."

"Are those made of mud, or what?"

"You can't tell about that now. Mud might have been used, but it would have washed away. You can see rectangular walls of rocks stacked up against a big boulder, or into the bank of the hill. I've dug down on some of the walls. They aren't very high. When they were used, they probably had poles holding up a roof of skins, or more poles on top with grasses and mud to give shelter from the sun. Most of the things the Indians left behind have been picked up. Rose Hill is easy to get to, and everybody comes here to look for arrowheads. So now, the only way to find anything is to dig."

"Did you find the arrowheads by digging?" asked Marylu.

Tim nodded, saying, "An arrowhead is small and easy to miss. I discovered Mom's strainer worked fine to sift through the stuff. She didn't think much of the idea, but finally she donated the strainer to the cause, and bought herself a new one. Well, here's the first wall." Tim jumped down from Sky. He looped the reins over a branch.

"Come on, I'll show you the rest," he said. He started climbing up the hill. Marylu tied Blue Girl and followed.

"Here," Tim began, and broke off. In front of him was a big mound of something tied up in a very un-Indian like tarpaulin. "Now, just who's big idea is this?" he demanded. "Looks as though somebody is fixing to camp on our property."

46

"That's an awful big bunch of stuff for campers," observed Marylu.

"It's a good thing we came out here. They could start squatting on our property, and first thing you know they'd claim it was theirs."

"It's a very new looking tarp," said Marylu. "Let's peek under it."

Tim lifted the edge of the tarp. On a metal box was printed GLOBE MINING CO. GLOBE, ARIZONA.

"Those mining men!" Tim whispered. "They're planning to drill here!"

"Oh, Tim, won't all the Indian ruins be torn up?"

"They can't do it! I'll talk to Dad. He'll stop them. Boy, it's sure lucky we came out here in time. Come on, I want to go find Dad."

Mounted, the young people rode fast to the ranch. When Tim saw Dutch out by the barn shoeing Jennie, he wasted no time coming to the point. Marylu heard him say, "Hey, Dad, those mining men are planning to drill on Rose Hill!"

"That's right," Dutch said without opening his mouth. Horseshoe nails were clamped between his teeth.

"You know about this?" Tim asked, surprised.

Dutch moved the nails, and said, "Of course. I took them there."

"Why there, Dad? You know the Indian ruins are there. Why didn't you take them some other place?"

"That's where they wanted to go." As though to end the conversation, Dutch put the nails back into his mouth, and pounded another nail into Jennie's hoof.

"That's our land and our Indian ruin! They can drill on the other side of the creek!"

Unmoved by Tim's agitation, Dutch pounded in the last nail, then tested around the shoe. He put Jennie's foot down, and gave her a whack of dismissal on the rump. She trotted away.

"Those are just some old Apache ruins that everybody has known about for years. Anything of value had been carted off long before we came here. I know you have had fun poking in them, Tim, but those mining men have been given permission, *by me,* to drill there."

"Why that spot, Dad? We've got lots of other places just as good."

"Well, Tim, they don't think so. They think there's mineral there, and that's where they want to drill."

Tim was stunned. "And . . . if they find something?"

"Then I guess they would stake a claim on it. You see, Son, we don't own the mineral rights. Under some of the old laws, the government didn't include mineral rights with a homestead, and this land was originally a homestead."

"Then these mining people could stake a claim, and come in here, and take the mineral right out of our own ground, and there's nothing we could do about it?"

"That's about the size of it, Tim."

"But that's not fair. That's a crazy law!"

"Maybe so," Dutch said mildly, "but until some of us people decide to do something about changing the law, we're going to have to put up with it."

"How do you stake a claim, anyway?" Tim asked.

"Well, you go down to the court house in Globe, and get some forms to fill out—."

"Then why don't we stake a claim before they do?"

"Oh, now, I can't do that," Dutch said, gathering his tools. "You have to make a discovery before you can file a claim; otherwise, the claim isn't good or valid."

"What kind of a discovery?"

"Oh, some mineral of value, gold, silver, copper, or whatever, and you have to be able to prove it, of course. Claims aren't as easy to make as you might think."

"But what if you did file one?"

"Well, the mining company could take it to court, and if I couldn't prove that I had made a real discovery, the claim would be branded invalid, that means no good, and—" He disappeared into the barn with his tools.

"Boy, how do you like that!" Tim said to Marylu. "Those guys are going to come in here and just take over the whole place."

"Your Dad needs the roads they're going to build," Marylu reminded him. "So, really, they're helping each other."

Tim didn't say any more, but his mind was made up to find some way whereby Dutch could stake a claim on Rose Hill that would be "good and valid."

7 THE LETTER

TIM HAD grown enthused over Marylu's idea of making a place for his Indian collection. "With people carting off relics, and mining men blasting them to bits, there won't be anything left before long," he said. "At least we can take care of what I have already found."

Marylu was sweeping cobwebs from the rafters. Everything in the shed had been sorted. Some was piled in an old trunk, to keep. Some had been removed to the barn. Most of it had been carried to the garbage pit. Tim had just taken the last load.

It was still early, and they figured if they hurried, they might have time to paint the shed before day's end. They had found paint in the shed while cleaning; two gallon cans nearly full, one of pale green and one of pale yellow, left over from painting the living room and front bedroom of the house. Tim didn't think there was enough to cover the old, dry boards. There was the red paint he had used on the signs, but that was enamel paint which wouldn't mix with the water paint in the big cans. He went looking for more, and found a small can of bright blue paint in the cupboard on the service porch. Then he climbed through the rail fence and struck out for the barn. Surely there would be some paint there.

Joe was lying in the sun by the pump house. Tim stopped beside him. "Hi, Joe, Old Buddy."

Joe spent most of his time licking his wounded leg. The swelling had gone down, but Joe wouldn't touch his paw to the ground. Tim wondered if his leg really was broken. He put out his hand to touch it, but Joe struggled out of reach, pulled himself up on his three legs, and lurched away.

"He'll never be my dog again," Tim thought sadly to himself, as he shuffled on to the barn to look for paint.

He poked about for some time, and finally he found some just the right color, bright orange. What bad luck there was so little of it. He hurried back to show it to Marylu.

"Boy, if we just had some more of this," he said, "it would be 'zingy'."

Marylu looked, and said, "Oh, Tim, what a horrible idea. No one could stand to come in here if we painted it that color. I can see you don't know much about colors and painting."

Tim put the orange paint with the other paint cans, saying, "Well, what we have here is all the paint on the ranch, and I know Mom and Dad won't let us buy any more for this old hole."

"I don't think any one of them will be enough to cover it," said Marylu. "I guess we could paint two walls yellow and two green."

"Those sissy colors!" Tim made a face. Then a thought came to him. "Hey, I know! Maybe we can paint each board a different color, an orange one, a green one, a yellow one, a blue one, over and over. Wow! That's it. That would be real 'zingy'."

"Oh, no!" said Marylu. "Not if I'm going to help."

"Tim," Mom called from the kitchen.

"Yes'um!" Tim answered, poking his head out the door of the shed.

"Before the mailman comes, will you and Marylu take this letter to the mailbox for me, please?" she asked.

"Sure, Mom. Come on, Marylu," said Tim.

While Tim went in for the letter, Marylu put the broom in the corner, and brushed cobwebs out of her hair. When he returned, he had the letter and two big hunks of fresh gingerbread which Mom had given him for them to eat on the way.

The mailbox was on the highway, about as far as two city blocks. They crossed the creek, climbed the bank, walked through a stand of junipers and then down a slope to the base of the road grade, to get to the mailbox. Then when he opened it, the mailman had already been and gone.

Tim pulled out the paper from Phoenix and a handful of letters and advertisements. He closed the box and sorted through the letters to see if anything was interesting. "Hey, coupons!" Tim said, holding the envelope up to the sun. "Lots of them!"

Marylu pulled at one of the envelopes. "What's this. Look! It's from the Museum. It's to you, Tim. It's your answer. Open it; hurry!"

Tim carried the letter to a stump, where he could sit and read in comfort. Ripping open the envelope, he looked inside. "There's no check," he said in a disappointed tone.

"Well, what does it say?" asked Marylu, standing beside him.

"It says: ' . . . The picture and the description indicate that the pot was not made by the Apaches. It would appear to be from the Sa— the Salado Culture. These people came into the area about 1250 A. D. and were there until about 1450 A. D. Why or how they disappeared is not fully understood. Lack of water, or the coming of the warlike Apache may have made them move away. Some may have stayed and intermixed with the Apaches. At any rate their pottery was distinctly their own. This pot was probably used for storing grain or water.

" 'If you will contact the Indian Research Center in Globe, or perhaps take your find into the Center, you may be able to obtain additional information. Mrs. Sara Starkweather is in charge there and will be most helpful in answering any further questions you may have about any finds. Very truly yours . . . ' He doesn't say whether or not it's worth anything," Tim said.

"Where did he say to take it, Tim?" asked Marylu.

"The Indian Research Center in Globe," Tim read again. "I didn't know there was such a place around here."

"And how old did he say it might be? 1250 A. D. from 19 . . . Good grief, Tim, that's over seven hundred years old. It must be worth something if it's that old."

"Oh, boy," exclaimed Tim. "Let's get home and see if anybody's going into town today. Maybe we can take the pot and go to that Research Center and find out how valuable it is." He ran up the slope toward the ranch house with Marylu close behind.

Mom was going grocery shopping, and she agreed to take Tim and Marylu to the Center. She called the Center and made an appointment with Mrs. Starkweather and explained about the pot. Tim decided he would tell her about the metate too, in case she would want to see it another time.

"I'll have to wash my hair and bathe," Marylu stated.

"Of course," said Mom. "Tim will have to clean up too. So you run along and have your bath first so you'll both be ready when I want to go."

Marylu left and Tim went out to the shed to wait

his turn. He wondered again how they could paint the shed with such a sorry lot of paint.

He guessed they would be lucky to have enough paint if it was all put together to do the job. That was it! He could put all the paint together. That ought to make a great color for sure.

He got a big oil can and dumped all the paint he had collected into it, and began to stir. The bright blue and red swirled into the mass of green and yellow. Yes siree, this was the ticket! No one had ever seen this color before, and no doubt about it, this was going to be a mighty 'zingy' color. But the longer he stirred, and the colors blended together, the less hopeful he felt.

At last he held up the stirring stick. What a nothing color, like washed out mud. He tried a brushful on the wall. It had no 'zing' at all. He spread on another brushful. What a mess!

"Oh, Tim!"

Tim looked up to see Marylu in the doorway. "Oh, oh," he thought to himself. "I guess she'll quit helping on the shed for sure."

"Where did you find that paint?" she asked.

"Find it?" repeated Tim trying hard to think of something to say so he wouldn't have to admit that he had used up all the paint there was.

Marylu said enthusiastically, "It's just the color we need. It'll make all the old things stand out and have real character. Where did you find it?"

Tim swallowed his surprise. He took a deep

breath and said, "Well, as a matter of fact, I mixed it from what was here."

"But how?" asked Marylu. "It's so perfect."

"Well," Tim continued, straightening up, "it wasn't exactly easy. You have to understand a few tricks about colors, you know. I'll just put these cans away and wash up the brush so I can go get ready. And someday when I have more time . . . I'll show you how I did it." He quickly gathered up the things and left the puzzled Marylu in the shed.

"How in the world did he manage to get just the right color?" she wondered.

8 THE RESEARCH CENTER

MRS. STARKWEATHER at the Research Center was a tall, gray-headed lady with merry eyes, who insisted on being called Mrs. Sara. She invited Marylu and Tim to remain at the Center while Mom shopped. That way, there would be time to see the various displays as well as discuss the pot.

"You must have had quite a task putting this together," Mrs. Starkweather said.

"Yes'um," said Tim, "we had a little trouble at first."

"We used masking tape to hold it together while the glue dried," Marylu explained.

"That was clever thinking, but a sand pile might have helped you even more," Mrs. Sara said.

"A sand pile?"

"Yes, as you fit the pieces together, the sand can be molded about them to hold them at just the right angle until the glue sets. Where did you find this, Tim?"

"It was sort of wedged in the branches of a tree.

I thought it was Apache pottery until the letter came from the Museum. A tree seems a strange place to find something seven hundred years old."

"I should think so," agreed Mrs. Sara. "But I would guess some prospector came across it and placed it in the tree, planning to get it later. Now only heaven could tell us where it came from, and that is one of the sad results when amateurs make finds. You see, the place where this pot originally belonged, might have yielded much more to a trained eye. It's very important to keep a record of the exact location of anything you find, and just how to find the place again."

Tim had been listening intently. "Write it down in a regular notebook, you mean?"

Mrs. Sara nodded. "You should record the date and any other useful information. Then you should put a tiny identifying number on your find to match a corresponding number in your notebook."

"I found a metate and mano, too, but not at the same place," Tim said.

"While metates were made by the Ancient Ones, later Indians found and used them, and moved them about the countryside. What might have been learned from knowing their original location has been lost."

Marylu brushed her hair back and spoke to Mrs. Sara. "The letter said that these Salado people were here before the Apaches."

"Yes, first there was the Hohokam. The word

59

'Hohokam' means 'those who have vanished.' Then the Salado people came."

"Did they have a war?" asked Tim.

"No, the Salado and the Hohokam apparently got along well, living side by side and sharing their knowledge. From the Hohokam, the Salado people learned about digging canals and irrigating crops so they could survive in this dry land. And from the Salado people, the Hohokam learned to build sturdier houses many stories high, to protect themselves from enemies. Evidently, all went well, with each type of culture sharing things to help the other and yet retaining separate customs and ways of making pottery and tools. Then those Old Ones or Ancient Ones, as they are called now, simply vanished from history."

"Don't we know why?" Tim asked.

"The coming of the Apache, perhaps; or maybe it was a great drought or flood that came, or maybe several things happened simultaneously. We're still trying to find out why and how the Ancient Ones disappeared."

Tim's interest in Mrs. Sara's story had nearly driven the thought of a bicycle from his mind. Now he said, "If this pot is that old, it ought to be valuable."

"Of course it's valuable, not in the money sense, perhaps, but in archaeological terms. If only we knew from where this really came! If we could find others like it still in their original position, we might unearth more of the secrets of the ancient tribes."

Vastly disappointed, Tim tried to keep his feelings from showing. "I guess it is interesting to find out about them. Still, those Indians can't teach us anything we don't already know. They were savages."

Mrs. Sara answered, "By our standards, they were not civilized. Yet they created beautiful and useful objects, and possibly they understood the laws of nature better than we do."

She stood up, brushing the wrinkles from her skirt. "The more we learn about the way they lived, the more we learn about ways we can live better. For instance, the first settlers drew their ideas for irrigating from these Old Ones. No, Tim, even now these ancient peoples can teach us many things."

Tim thought about what was to happen on Rose Hill. He wondered what might yet be learned from the Indians who had lived there, if only the ruins were spared.

"Now let me show you two around the Center." Mrs. Sara led the way through the several rooms, each representing a different era of human habitation in the area. Marylu was spellbound before the dioramas. Tim was interested in everything. He made mental notes of all he heard and saw, thinking that he could use some of these ideas in his museum at home. He was so busy looking and making plans, he almost forgot that another plan for getting his bike had fallen through.

"This room, we have given over to the Apache," Mrs. Sara said. "We think they arrived about 1450, probably beating Columbus by a few years. The Apaches were nomadic and very warlike."

As Tim was passing through the door, he stopped so short that Marylu bumped into him.

"Oh, Tim, I'm sorry," she said and stepped aside to see what had brought him to such a quick halt. Tim went on staring at a figure confronting him.

"Why, Tim, what's the matter?" Mrs. Sara asked. "That's just Old Hawk," she laughed.

"Old Hawk?" Tim almost choked on the words.

"You see, we wanted to show the aboriginal dress of the Apache. Someone found this old store dummy which we have fixed up. I thought it worked out rather well."

The tall dummy had a wig of long black hair. He was dressed in breeches and a tunic made from some kind of skin, and wore knee-length moccasins having a disk of skin turned up in front. Lines painted on the face gave it a fierce look. His eyes gleamed in the light, making him look alive and ready to use the axe which he held in his raised right hand.

"Why did you call him Old Hawk?"

Mrs. Sara was obviously startled by Tim's fervency. She answered, "Many years ago, there used to be an old Indian around here by that name. He was rather strange, but everyone knew him and got used to him being about. Don't you think his name

62

is appropriate for our Indian in the Apache Room?"

"Yes'um," Tim nodded his head emphatically. "It really is. It's just about perfect, I'd say." He took a deep breath and moved away from Old Hawk's overpowering presence.

Marylu whispered, "I guess horses aren't the only things that Old Hawk spooks. You're white as chalk."

Mrs. Sara was speaking. "You know, Tim, this is primarily a research center. It isn't a museum in the usual sense. But occasionally we have an open house and let everyone who is interested see the displays. We are planning to have an open house next week. I wonder if you would like to display your pot."

"Display it?"

"I don't want to encourage amateurs taking up archaeology as a hobby, but yours is an interesting specimen."

"Maybe we could display it with a sign explaining the things amateurs should do when they find something," Marylu suggested.

"That's a splendid idea!"

Mrs. Sara gave them supplies, and while Marylu printed the sign, Tim helped with preparations for the open house. He carried boxes, moved tables, cleaned glass cases and dusted shelves. By the time Mom returned, Tim had accomplished quite a bit, or Mrs. Sara apparently thought so.

"This boy is a big help," she said to Mom. "I

didn't think we would have everything done in time, but with this bit of special help, I think perhaps we will."

"It was fun," Tim said.

Instead of driving straight back to the ranch, Mom parked near the county court house, saying she had to pick up clothes at the cleaners. Tim always hated to sit and wait for Mom. The nearby court house gave him a better idea. "Come on, Marylu, let's go get some forms."

"Some forms? What forms?" she asked, puzzled.

"Don't you remember Dad saying you had to get forms to file a claim?"

"Oh, Tim." Marylu climbed wearily out of the car. "What are you cooking up now? You know your Dad said he couldn't stake a claim that would mean anything."

"He might have overlooked something. It won't hurt to get the forms and have them handy."

Marylu followed Tim, deciding she might as well stand by and try to keep him from doing anything foolish. They were back in the car by the time Mom came out of the cleaning shop.

"I'm sorry I took so long," she said. "There was such a line and only one girl at the counter."

"Oh, we didn't mind," said Tim. "It didn't seem like any time at all."

Mom turned to look at him. She wondered if she should take his temperature when they got home.

9 OPEN FOR BUSINESS

TIM AND Marylu were kept busy for the next several days. First there was the shed to paint. They spent one long day covering the old boards. On the inside at least, the shed took on a bright, new look.

Whenever he had the chance, Tim studied the claim forms and the booklet that the man at the Mineral Resources office had given him at the court house.

One day in his room he asked Marylu, "What does this mean, d-i-s-c-r-e-t-i-o-n?"

"What? Let me see it."

"It says here that anyone can stake a claim who is a citizen and has reached that age," and he showed her the word.

Marylu thought a minute. "I guess it means when you're old enough to keep a secret."

"Then I guess I can stake that claim myself. I'm a citizen, and I sure can keep a secret."

"Oh, are you on that again?" she groaned.

"Look, I've gone all over these forms, and I've read

65

all through this book, and I think I can pull it off. If it doesn't work, there's no harm done. And it just might save the Indian ruins on Rose Hill."

He slapped the booklet down on his desk. "I'm going to stake it out now. Are you going to help me, or not?"

Marylu made a face but she got up to follow Tim. "You're just wasting your time. It can't work. You'll find out."

Tim filled out two of the forms, placing one in a tin can. The other he put in an envelope to mail to the recording office at the court house.

The rest of that day, he and Marylu spent on Rose Hill, measuring and locating his claim. They marked the corners with piles of rock. Beneath a rock monument in the center was placed the tin tobacco can containing the copy of the form for filing the claim, with the measurements and locations of the corners entered in the proper places.

They returned to the house late in the afternoon. Because Tim thought it was necessary, they were careful not to mention what they had been doing.

"I'll have to prove I've reached the age of discretion," Tim explained earnestly. Marylu wondered if the word might have another meaning than the one she had given it.

The next two days were spent in finishing the shed. With some difficulty, they managed to mount an old saddle on one wall in spread-eagle fashion. Around this they arranged an old branding iron, a bridle, a couple of riding bits, some horseshoes, a lantern, some old chaps; and they topped off the display with an assortment of equipment used for camping during roundup: the big iron skillet, the gallon-sized tin coffeepot, and the Dutch oven. Then Tim began carrying all of his relics out of his room.

On little shelves between the wall studs in one section of the end wall, Tim placed his rock collection. He taped names on the edge of the shelves . . . QUARTZ . . . JASPER . . . SANDSTONE . . . FELDSPAR . . . PETRIFIED WOOD. On the next section he carefully hung his collection of birds' nests. On the next the driftwood was attached. On the last section he fastened a board to which he had glued the arrowheads and potsherds he had found.

While Tim worked on his wall, Marylu worked on a section of another wall. She was determined to make a diorama such as she had seen at the Research Center. She mixed color from her tubes of water colors with some of the wall paint, and soon had a vivid picture mural beginning with the ancient Hohokam, showing the coming of the Salado peoples, the Apaches, and finally of the mountain men and the settlers. From bits of wire, strips of newspaper, and paste, she molded tiny animals and people. After they were dry and painted, she arranged them on the braces between the wall studs in front of her picture mural. Her completed diorama had a true three-dimensional effect.

Tim made a table using planks and sawhorses,

which he put against the wall beneath his shelves. On this he carefully placed the metate and the mano.

"It looks a little bare, doesn't it?" he asked.

Mom answered from the doorway. "But what a relief it is. Why, your room looked so empty, I decided to give it a good cleaning."

"Aw, Mom, what did you do that for? There was still lots of stuff in there I wanted."

"Well, I can't imagine what it could have been," said Mom.

"What about my popsickle sticks?"

"Well, I did take them out," Mom admitted. "But they are still in their paper bag on top of the garbage can. What on earth do you want with used popsickle sticks?"

"I've been saving them for a whole year, so I'd have enough to make a log cabin."

Mom laughed. "This old shed is good for something after all. At least you have a place for building log cabins, or anything else you like."

Dutch joined the group in the shed. "You kids have done a bang up job with this old fire trap. Marylu, your picture is a true work of art, and I think it deserves a reward of some kind. How would you like to have a roping lesson?"

"Oh, that would be neat." Marylu jumped up. She had wanted to learn to use a rope for ever so long, and Uncle Dutch was an authority on the subject. "Do you mean right this minute?" she asked hopefully.

"Sure, come on," Dutch said. Marylu followed him happily to the tack room for ropes.

"Tim, it's marvelous how nice the shed looks. I'm very pleased," Mom said as she turned to go. "But you had better pick up the tools you were using and put them away, and why don't you clean Marylu's brushes for her too," she suggested.

"Oh sure," thought Tim. "Everybody just goes off to have a fine time, leaving me to pick up everything and clean it and put it away."

He poked Marylu's brushes into water and swished them about until the water foamed. He picked up the tools and the other things and put them all away. When he turned to observe the final results, he thought again that the metate looked lonesome on its sawhorse table.

"That table needs something more on it," he decided, thinking there would be no time for him and Marylu to find more things if she intended to go on roping fence posts. That was a girl for you. She had started the whole idea about making the shed into a museum. Now she had forgotten it all just to go play with a rope.

He stomped out to the corral, where Marylu was listening to Dutch explain how to hold the rope. Tim saddled Sky while he waited for a chance to speak to her.

Tim said, "I'm going to look for more relics. The museum isn't much of a museum yet, you know."

He put his hands on his hips, and his eyes challenged her. "You going to come along?"

"Oh, Tim," she said in dismay. "I can't go now." She carefully coiled the rope around her left hand. "Why don't we wait until tomorrow?"

Tim said nothing. He turned on his heel and led Sky back to the house, tying him to the rail fence.

Marylu didn't care about the museum anymore. That was plain enough. And she certainly had made it clear how she felt about his wanting a bike. If that was the way she felt, that was her business. He guessed he would just take care of his own.

He got his hammer, and the two signs stacked behind the shed. He nailed ADMISSION $1.00 on the inside of the far door and WRELICS OF THE WEST on the outside by the front door. Now he was open for business.

He went into the rock house where the big freezer was and where Mom kept lots of other supplies. He found a bag of apples. He stuffed one in his shirt, and began to eat another. Mom heard the door of the rock house slam.

"Now, Tim, if you are going off, be back in time for supper," she called.

"Okay, Mom, I will." Later he was to remember how easily and quickly he had promised her.

Joe was watching by the back door, his hurt paw mid-air. Tim stooped to rub his ears. "You want to come with me, Joe?"

Joe hung his head. "Come on. Let's go together the way we used to," Tim begged. He felt very alone.

But Joe moved away with his clumsy, three-legged gait. He stopped beside the trumpet vine and watched Tim as he mounted Sky and started off.

Tim rode a long time, feeling very sorry for himself. He leaned over and rubbed Sky on the neck. He guessed it was not bad having a horse of his own. No one seemed to care about what he did, and certainly no one else cared whether he ever got a bike or not. But he still had Sky. He felt he might have been a little disloyal to Sky, wanting the bike so much.

Soon he began to think about the business at hand, which was to look for more relics. He wished he could find a place where the Old Ones had lived. The big pot had originally come from such a place. He thought about the Indian, Old Hawk, and wondered if he had camped and roamed in these particular hills. Probably Old Hawk would have known all the places where the Old Ones had lived.

Tim passed the manzanita thicket. From here on there were high cliffs and deep ravines with creeks cutting through. He had heard that there were even caves.

The terrain became rougher as Tim traveled over a series of long, sloping ridges, climbing higher and higher. Presently, there was no higher ground. He could see a blue horizon far ahead of him. The

71

sun was beginning to sink. He jumped down from Sky and looped his reins over a bush.

"Wow, look at that drop. This is a real cliff we're on," Tim remarked to Sky.

There was a flat area of several acres at the base of the cliff. The ridges sloped downward and away much the same as on the side Tim on Sky had climbed. There was a little dry wash running through the flat.

"Boy," thought Tim to himself, "if years ago, that wash had water, this would be the sort of spot the Indians would have used for growing their crops. If none lived around here, that was just because they didn't find the place."

He picked up a stick and chewed on it thoughtfully as he studied the view before him. "I wonder if Old Hawk ever came around here," he thought.

Down and directly in front of Tim was a narrow shelf of earth protruding from the cliff face. It ran around to the left and disappeared in the rocks and brush running up to the crown of the ridge.

His curiosity roused, Tim knelt on the edge of the cliff and strained to see if any of the rock chips were of flint, such as arrowheads were made from. He saw an arrowhead, then another! Tim pushed himself out a little farther to see better. A rock gave way, and down he went.

10 THE CAVE

Tim blinked his eyes, which finally focused. He was looking at blue sky and the rocky edge of the cliff above him. Everything was quiet. He could see, and he could breathe, and he was no longer dropping through the air. His right hand hurt, though.

He found he was tightly grasping a scraggly branch of a catclaw bush, which had managed somehow to grow out of the sparse soil on the cliff face. Gingerly, he brought his hand back and examined its flesh. Some thorns remained in his palm.

Tim sat up. He was on the ledge. Had it not been there, the fall would have killed him. Of course, he wouldn't have fallen in the first place except for his interest in the ledge.

Tim's legs worked all right, no broken bones, but his scratches and skinned places were beginning to sting. He picked at the thorns in his hand and sucked on the punctures to make them bleed. All the time his real attention was on the spot where he had seen the flint chips.

He saw hard black and brown flint rocks and some red jasper, all of a type once used to make arrowheads. He picked up two beautiful arrowheads of obsidian, the smokey-colored glass rock of Apache tears. So busy was he hunting these finds, he failed to notice how dark it was getting, until he began having trouble discerning jasper from obsidian.

"I guess I'd better find a way out of here before it gets too dark," Tim said aloud.

He scanned the towering cliff wall a good ten feet above him. No way out there, and very cautiously, he looked over the edge. "Wow, about another thirty feet!" Tim's eyes followed the ledge to the right. It was a sheer drop. To the left it disappeared behind some brush which looked impassable.

He felt hungry, and remembering, unbuttoned his pocket for the apple he had put there. Munching thoughtfully, he studied the mass of bushes. One bush grew just above the ledge and another just below. Their branches were small where they crossed on the ledge. In front of the bushes was a rock about as big as a milk bucket.

"If I rolled that out of the way and broke those small branches, I bet I could get through there," Tim said to himself.

He gave his apple a final turn, skinning it down to the seed, and tossed it over the edge. With his good hand, he took a firm hold on the bush near its base, and tugged. The bush was solidly attached, and would give him support while he tried to shove the big rock out of the way. Planting both feet against the back of the rock, he began pushing. Slowly, it moved to the edge. Tim gave it a last shove with one foot and it thundered down the side of the cliff hitting here and there, splintering other rocks as it went.

He broke away the branches arching over the path. In the dusky light, he could see how the ledge twisted around a curve of the cliff. Carefully, he crawled through and around the curve—and stopped. In front of him yawned a big opening in the cliff. It was a cave.

Inside the cave was as large as a shallow room. At this point the ledge was wider. Low rocks along its edge indicated that at one time there might have been a wall there. Some holes high on the sides of the opening suggested that poles might have supported a roof of some kind.

"Wow, look at that!" Outlined faintly in the fading light were three huge pots and two smaller bowl-shaped pottery pieces. Tim scrambled to inspect them. The large pots were rough and of a brownish color. One had a long neck. Two of the smaller pots were rough and brownish, but the outside of the third was a deep red, and—

"Great jumping coyotes!" Tim said. Inside the colored basin was a black and white design. He could make out black triangular shapes forming the head of a bird, with white squares holding black square dots for eyes.

He picked up his find. On one edge a small bit was broken out. Along the broken edge was a half moon of what appeared to have been a hole, so perfectly round it could only have been made by a drilling tool.

Carefully, he moved the other pots. He found two stones shaped and grooved in such a way that he was sure they were axe heads. But now he realized it had grown very dark.

Again he searched for a means of getting up or down. He could see no more than a few feet away. "Hey," he yelled out to the darkness. "Hey, can anyone hear me?"

He listened for an answer. He got one. Sky whinnied! "Poor old Sky," thought Tim, "tied to a bush and nothing to eat." He sat down and rubbed his face.

"Boy, what a dope. I've fixed things really good this time," he said to himself.

Tim decided he might as well make the best of this and try to sleep it out. At least the night was warm. With rocks bordering the ledge, there was certainly no chance of rolling off. In the morning he could figure out something. He lay down just outside the mouth of the cave.

At home everyone would be sitting down to a supper of chicken dumplings and gravy, or maybe a big bean pot with green chilies roasted and peeled. Tim sighed. His stomach was very empty. He swallowed a big gulp of air and tried to forget his hunger.

He lay quietly for some time and listened to Sky whinnying for his supper. Then he heard a noise. It was so stealthy, at first he thought he might have been mistaken. Then he heard it again, from behind him in the cave. He had thought that was just one shallow room, and in his excitement, had not noticed whether there were other rooms beyond the shadows.

Without making any noise Tim turned to look into the cave's black mouth. Two round, glowing balls looked back at him. Tim began to scoot quietly backward along the ledge on his stomach.

11 OLD HAWK

Tim moved backward on the ledge until he came to the tunnel he had made through the bushes. He dared not go farther for fear of exciting the occupant of the cave by his noise. This was a likely spot for a mountain lion, and Tim tried to think what he would do if one started toward him.

His hand searched the ledge for rocks to throw. His fingers pried loose a round, flat object. He hoped he wouldn't need to throw that. Its feel in his hand made him think it might be an artifact. He pocketed it.

The glowing eyes continued to stare in his direction. Perhaps he could push the animal off the ledge, provided he could find a way to keep from falling off himself. He groped for the branch of the bush that had supported him earlier, when he rolled the big rock over the edge. He found it and tightened his fingers around it. Very slowly, without making any noise, he reversed his position so that his booted feet were in front of him. He could do some good kicking if necessary. Now he was ready. All he could do was wait.

To Tim, it seemed that hours passed. His hand cramped, and he lowered it to rest. He became drowsy and nearly fell asleep. Remembering the thirty foot drop, he jerked himself awake, biting his cheeks on the inside to keep alert. The unblinking eyes stared on.

Above the hills, across the flat to the east, a tip of moon appeared. Rising, it painted the cliff face with misty light which spread to the flat below. The glowing animal eyeballs faded.

There was movement. A pebble rolled down. Tim blinked and tried to adjust his eyes. Something black was coming out of the shadows. He gripped the branch, braced for battle.

"Ah, it's nothing but a dumb skunk!"

The striped animal ignored him and ambled away. Sniffing along, picking its own secret path, it disappeared around the cliff front on the other side. Tim took a deep breath and spat over the edge.

"Boy, even a dumb skunk can get out of here," he muttered as he crawled back along the ledge to the cave. "So why can't I?" Yawning, he stretched out to sleep, one arm upflung to ward off the brightness of moonglow.

Perhaps he was too tired to sleep. He began to wonder how many animals had used the cave for a home. He imagined all kinds of animals lurking in the shadows of the cave.

He remembered the round, flat object he had found while hunting something to throw. He brought it out of his pocket but was too exhausted to give it even a cursory examination. It felt oddly warm in his hand, even comforting.

Holding the object which Indians had made turned his thoughts to them and their ways. They had lived in this cave. They had faced dangers and difficulties. They had endured. He could too.

Those pots he had found in the cave—had they been made by the Ancient Ones? Perhaps for a thousand years, the pots had waited for someone to come along and find them. Perhaps Old Hawk had found them before Tim had, but he wouldn't have told anyone. He would have kept his secret. That had been Old Hawk's way.

Suddenly Tim remembered the signs he had posted in the hope of getting money from the mining men. His idea had seemed such a good one, but now he felt that what he had planned was sneaky.

"Funny," he thought to himself. "Out here, alone, I feel different about a lot of things." Then he drifted into sleep.

"You, boy, I think you like all white men. You have bad head."

Tim sat up, blinking. Who was talking to him? Tim's heart seemed to jump a beat. In the pale light, he clearly saw a very tall Indian. His clothing was the kind that Apaches used to wear, even to the high knee boots that folded down at the top.

Tim swallowed. "You talking to me . . . sir?"

The Indian scowled and nodded. "You here. I here. Nobody else here."

Tim looked about. "No . . . no, sir, there sure isn't," Tim agreed, mightily wishing that someone were.

"I say you have bad head like all the rest."

Tim gulped. "I don't understand."

"I Old Hawk," the big, deep voice echoed. "I live long time, and I see many things for many years. I learn about white man."

Tim opened his mouth but nothing would come out.

"You take away Indian pots?" asked Old Hawk.

Tim swallowed again. It seemed his voice would never come. "Ye . . . yes, sir, I . . . I aim to take very good care of them!"

"Why you want Indian pots?" Old Hawk's voice seemed to boom out of every rock on the mountain-side.

"Well sir, well, as a matter of fact . . . " Tim found he didn't like to say this. "I . . . I want a bike!" he burst out in forced admission.

"Indian pots? Bike?" Old Hawk said inquiringly.

"Sir, you see, I figure lots of folks would pay money to see them—"

"You want Indian pots and Indian things, just for

getting money?" Old Hawk's eyes flashed in the dim light.

Tim squirmed in his dirt bed. He remembered what his Dad had said about trapping mountain lions for their bounty, just to buy a bike.

"Oh . . . oh, no sir," he stuttered. "I . . . I really like Indian things. I . . . I like to know about them." When he said it, Tim realized this was true.

Old Hawk spoke again. "The yucca grew by the white man's house. It had fruit for eating and leaves for weaving ropes and sandals, and roots for making soap. The white man dig it up and kill it, and throw it away. He miss many good things because he have bad head."

Tim knew yucca plants had been useful to the Indian. Had the white settlers overlooked something good?

"White man cut trees and clear away the bushes, and the wild things move away. The water run off and the streams dry up. No beauty is left but the sunset, which he cannot reach."

Tim's palms were damp as he tried to answer Old Hawk. "Th . . . the white men make many real nice things, too."

When Old Hawk nodded, his black hair swung about his face. "But can white man listen to the wind? Does he know what the seasons will bring, by watching the small creatures? White man cannot be still to know. The Indian knows." Tim guessed that what Old Hawk said might be true.

"You have good eye, like Indian. But you have bad head, like white man," Old Hawk said.

"Yes, sir, I . . . I guess I'm kind of mixed up," admitted Tim.

Old Hawk said, "The piece you hold in your hand was mine. When I small boy, my mother make it for me. My father get metal from the white man and give it to her to make that to wear around my neck. She make the pictures. She come from the Old Ones, and she very wise."

"I guess you want it back," Tim said, holding it out.

"You keep, maybe you be wise. My mother say when she give it to me, 'What this means is what you must search for!' I grown man before I know what she tells me, that the Old Ones were wise because they give to each other, not fight and take away. You look. You think. Maybe you know."

Tim found he was sitting up in bright sunlight, the round, flat object still warming his hand.

"Wow, what a dream!" Or had it been a dream? A shiver ran between his shoulder blades.

He examined the piece Old Hawk had claimed was his. It was a little larger than a half dollar piece, worn-looking, dull in color. Its edges were fluted, and faintly etched into the surface, he could make out a bird . . . the sun . . . and some straight slanting lines like rain. It had a hole in one end. Nothing had been through that hole in a long time.

Suddenly Sky whinnied, and just as suddenly Tim

heard in the distance the familiar "Whoop! Whoop! Whoop!" of Joe's barking.

Tim dropped the Indian ornament into his back pocket, and let out a yell. "Yeh-hoo! Joe! Yeaaa . . . Joe!" And he whistled, and he yelled, and he whistled.

12 THE RESCUE

"WHOOP! WHOOP! Whoop!" Joe was getting closer. Sky whinnied long and loud. Tim watched the cliff edge above for a first glimpse of Joe.

"Come on, Joe!" Tim shouted.

Joe's head appeared above, cocked inquiringly. When Tim moved, Joe spotted him, and dancing and bobbing along the edge, he whined his joy and relief.

Tim tried to calm the excited dog. "Careful, Joe. You don't want to land down here too." Even with the aid of the morning sunlight, Tim could see no easy way to solve his problem of getting off the cliff. Then Tim heard a faint whistle.

Joe turned away from the cliff edge. "Whoop! Whoop! Whoop!"

Tim heard the sounds of horses. "Hey, Dad, here I am!" Tim shouted over and over.

A head appeared at the cliff edge. It was Jim Swartz, a neighbor. "Well, as I live and breathe! Here he is, and in one piece."

Tim called, "You helping Dad look for me, Jim?"
Then his father's head came into view alongside
Jim's.

"Are you all right, Son?" Dutch asked.

"Sure, Dad, just some scratches. Boy, is it good
to see you! I was beginning to wonder if I would
ever get off this cliff."

"Well, we'll fix that up. Just sit tight. We'll get
some rope." They disappeared from the edge.

"Well, finally the lost has been found." This time,
it was Marylu. Even from this distance, Tim
thought she seemed tired.

She called to him, "Tim, how did you ever get
down there in the first place?"

"It was easier and quicker than you would think,"
Tim muttered to himself. Aloud, he said, "Wait 'til
you see what I've found! Here, I'll show you." Tim
scrambled back to the cave for the bowl with the
beautiful design.

"How's this for a find?" he asked, holding it up for
Marylu to see.

"Oh, Tim! It's gorgeous!"

"There are four more pieces not so fancy, and
some stone axe heads and arrowheads. I really hit
the jackpot this time. Boy, wait until we get these
in our museum."

"*Our* museum?" echoed Marylu. Both her look
and her tone struck him as odd. Before he could
question her, Dutch reappeared, a coil of rope over
his arm.

"Sky is really sucking in the water up here. I expect you could use some yourself, Son. Put this around your waist, fasten it, and hold on."

Tim held up the bowl with the design. "Dad. See this!"

"Hey, that is real pretty," Dutch said.

"And there's more," said Tim. "We've got to get them up first." He was already working with the rope to form a secure basket to carry the Indian bowl to the top of the cliff.

"Okay, Dad, pull her up!"

He watched long enough to see that his prize was safely on its way, then hurried back for the rest of the things. When all the pottery was raised, Dutch lowered a canvas bag, and in it Tim placed the smaller things he had found, the chips and arrowheads and the stone axe heads.

Finally, Tim tied himself into the rope, and was lifted carefully from his ledge to safety.

Before Tim could untangle himself, Joe was on him, licking his face, whining frantically, trying to reassure himself that it really was Tim.

"Oh, you cotton-picking dog, are you trying to smother me?" Tim hugged the wriggling Joe as they rolled over and over.

"Don't you want something to eat?" Marylu asked.

"I may have to eat this dog to get him off me." When Tim sat up, Joe backed away wagging from neck to tail. He was standing on all four legs, too.

"Hey, look at Joe," Tim said, accepting from

Marylu some cold roast beef and a canteen of water.

"All he needed was a little shock treatment, I guess, and your getting lost provided that," Marylu said. "He tracked you here. Without Joe, we wouldn't have known what direction to take."

The men had finished tying the pots and bowls onto the saddles, and were ready to start home. Tim took a last swig of water. How good it tasted, after the dry, hungry hours on the ledge. After checking his cinch, he hung the canteen over the saddlehorn and mounted with the others. They started off, Joe trailing.

"Now tell us all about it," said Dutch.

Tim told the whole story, only leaving out the part about the dream of Old Hawk, if dream it had been.

"Well, that kept you out of mischief for a few hours anyway," Jim Swartz said when Tim finished his story.

"You've found some interesting-looking things," Dutch said. "I don't approve of your method of coming across them, though. Falling off cliffs is doing it the hard way. Do you know that none of us had a wink of sleep last night, worrying about you?"

No wonder Marylu seemed tired!

"What do you plan to do with your finds?" Dutch was asking.

"I'll put them in the shed with my other stuff."

"You mean in the WRELICS OF THE WEST museum, ADMISSION $1.00?" Dutch asked.

"I was just trying to earn some extra money, so

I could get my bike before I'm about ninety years old," Tim said defensively.

"Is trying to dupe folks a good way?"

"They would have got something for their money," Tim said half-heartedly.

"If you weren't duping them, then you must have felt that what they got for their money was worth a dollar to them," Dutch said.

"Sure I did."

"If you felt it was worth a dollar, you would have put the sign where it could be seen by people before they went in."

"Hey, now, here is a boy out to make his first million," Jim Swartz said. Their neighbor sounded admiring, but Tim was ashamed of himself.

Dutch said in a kindly tone, "Even if it was right, you wouldn't be allowed to earn money by exhibiting those, Tim."

"Why not?" Tim protested, turning in his saddle to confront this new challenge.

"Well, you see, they don't belong to you."

"They don't? But I found them!"

"Tim, this land happens to be government-leased. So the things you found will have to be turned over to the proper authorities."

"Such as—?" Tim demanded.

"Well, I expect your friend at the Research Center might qualify," said Dutch. "I'm going to town tomorrow to pick up a part for the Cat. You can take them in then."

Tim on Skyrocket plodded along in silence. Everything had backfired for him. In spite of being tired and dirty and hungry from his night's ordeal, he had been happy and excited over the Indian finds; for themselves and not just because he wanted a bike. But now the excitement was gone, and he felt all his miseries at once.

Jim Swartz said to Dutch, "I meant to ask you, have the mining men found something on Rose Hill?"

"Not that I know of. Why?"

"Where they want to drill is right next to my piece, you know. I was over by that fence line the other day, and I noticed markers laid out and other indications of a claim on your place. Haven't they said anything to you?"

"Not a word," said Dutch. "I wonder what's going on."

Tim had been lagging behind. He closed his ears to the talk, saying to himself, "I didn't hear a thing. I don't know what they're talking about. Not now anyway. Not now, for sure." Enough things had gone wrong for one day.

He pulled up and waited for Marylu. Maybe telling her about the encounter with Old Hawk would bring back some of the happy excitement he had felt. But Marylu, usually such a sympathetic listener, seemed uninterested in Tim's story, which she dismissed as merely a dream. "Or maybe it's *me* she's not interested in," Tim thought, feeling sorry for himself. After such an adventure, what a letdown this was!

Mom met the party in the yard. Her first words to her son were, "Get out of those dirty clothes, and take a bath! If you forget and sit on something, you'll ruin it."

One minute, he was a big discoverer sending re-covered treasures up a cliff with the help of grown men; and the next, he had to be told to take a bath, like a little kid. Tim bent and rubbed Joe's ears, thinking that he had his dog back anyhow. The tumble over the cliff had accomplished at least that much.

13 A VALUABLE MINERAL

TIM HAD followed carefully his Dad's instructions about packing the pots and bowls he had found in the cave, for removal to the Research Center. The pieces were safely nested in old newspapers, and he had taken care to number each one. The numbers were listed in his notebook, with accompanying details.

After a good night's sleep, things were looking brighter to Tim. He managed to work up a small excitement of anticipation over what Mrs. Sara would say when she saw his new finds.

Marylu shared Tim's early breakfast. She was riding into Globe with Tim and Dutch in order to stay overnight with her friend, Jane. To Tim, Marylu's manner still seemed distant and strange. Perhaps she merely had her mind filled with thoughts of the visit to her friend.

Dutch came to the back door just as Tim and Marylu were finishing breakfast. *"Buenos tardes, compadre,"* Dutch said. "That's quite a claim you've staked for yourself over on Rose Hill."

"Yes, sir," Tim said, wishing his father hadn't learned about that quite so soon.

Dutch sighed. "I appreciate your trying to save those Indian ruins, but as I told you before, a claim isn't valid unless you have made a discovery of some valuable mineral."

"Yes, sir," agreed Tim. "I think I have."

"Have what?" asked Dutch.

"Made a discovery of a valuable mineral," Tim explained.

Dutch rubbed his chin. "Okay, show me a piece of this mineral you've found."

Tim went to his room. When he returned, he was holding something in his hand, which he opened for Dutch to see.

"Arrowheads!" Dutch snorted.

"Found them right in the middle of my claim," declared Tim.

"But that's not a valuable mineral, Tim."

"It's mineral, isn't it?"

"Yes."

"And it's valuable, too, though maybe not in a money sense." Tim spoke carefully. He was trying to remember Mrs. Sara's exact words. "In an archaeo-logical sense, my find is valuable."

Dutch laughed. "But that isn't what they had in mind, Tim."

Tim pulled the well-worn booklet from his pocket and read from it. "It says here a mineral is any in-or-gan-ic sub-stance found in nature, having sufficient value apart from the surrounding earth to be mined, quarried, OR extracted for its own sake or use." Tim looked up at his Dad. "That's true about the arrowheads."

Dutch wagged his head thoughtfully. "You filed this at the recorder's office?" Tim nodded. "Those mining men are going to find about a dozen reasons why your claim won't hold. They have been in this business a long time, you know. Just the same, it's a whale of a good try," Dutch said, seeming somewhat proud of Tim.

Then he spoiled it all by adding, "Anyhow, they'll have a good laugh."

Carrying his boxes to load into the car, Tim decided he was a little tired of being laughed at. Lately he seemed to have developed a talent for doing things folks found very funny. In fact, it seemed that he became ridiculous whatever he tried to do. He finished with his boxes and went to see if Marylu was ready.

"I'll carry it," she said coldly as Tim reached for her traveling case.

"What's eating you?" he asked.

"You know good and well! I told you that I wouldn't help in the shed if you were going to use those sneaky signs. You hid the signs to make me think you had changed your mind about that. Then the minute all the work is done, up they go." She picked up her traveling case and stormed out to the car.

94

Tim started after her. He should have known she would be angry about that. With everything else going on, he hadn't stopped to think about how she might be feeling. And maybe he really hadn't been fair with her.

The ride to town was a quiet one. Dutch looked from Tim to Marylu, but said nothing. When he let Marylu out at Jane's house, the goodbyes were barely heard.

At the Research Center, Dutch helped Tim carry in the boxes. Mrs. Sara hurried to meet them. "Tim, how on earth do you do it?" she asked when she heard about the new find. "How do you know where to go and where to look?"

Tim scratched his head. "Gee, I don't know," he said.

"Well, you certainly have a special knack for making finds. Did you record these in a notebook as I asked you to do?"

"Yes'um."

As they opened the boxes with Dutch's help, Tim told her about the fall from the cliff and then finding the cave. "Did the Salado people make these?" he asked.

"They did indeed. They are very nice ones, too," Mrs. Sara said. "I would like to see that cave."

Tim looked dubiously at her lined face and white hair. "It's an awfully long way. You have to go by horseback," he said.

"Fine," said Mrs. Sara. "Maybe your father has a horse I could use."

"We'd be glad to fix you up with one," Dutch said.

Remembering the thirty foot drop of the cliff, Tim said, "I don't think you could get down there."

She laughed and said, "I wouldn't try to the way you did. I might even show you a trick or two about going up and down cliffs."

Mrs. Sara took the bowl with the design in her hands. "Remember, I told you we might really learn important things about these people if we could just find relics in their original location. It sounds as if you have surely found such a place. The Salado people buried their dead, often under the floor of the places where they lived. Their custom was to bury very fine pieces of handiwork, so you see why I want to go to your cave."

"Jeepers, I want to go back myself!" Tim said.

He showed her the small half moon of a hole that he had wondered about on the bowl with the design. "Doesn't this look as if it had been made on purpose?"

"It was," Mrs. Sara said. "That is the way they mended their pottery. They would drill a hole in the pot at the proper place and another in the broken piece, and then tie them together with leather thongs." Mrs. Sara gently placed the bowl back into the box. "We must add these to your display for the open house."

96

Tim and Dutch carried the boxes to the display.

"Oh my, this will never work," said Mrs. Sara in dismay. "This case is much too small to show them properly. Would you have time before Saturday to change to a larger case?"

Tim turned to his Dad, who said, "As a matter of fact, I think your mother plans to come in early to shop tomorrow, and then pick up Marylu in the afternoon. You'd have plenty of time to work on it."

"Oh, that would be fine," exclaimed Mrs. Sara. "Maybe you can help us with some other things as well. How about it, Tim?"

"Yes, ma'am. I'll come. I'd like to."

Of course this was a poor bet for earning money to buy a bike. The bike would just have to wait. A lot of people would see his display at the open house; also, interesting things were going on at the Center, and Tim wanted to be a part of it.

That night at the supper table, Tim told Mom and Grandpa Cone about the open house at the Research Center, and the bigger display that he would have.

"Well, well," said Grandpa Cone, "are you planning to charge admission to this, or can I leave my bankroll at home when I go to look?"

Tim felt his ears getting red. He grinned and looked sideways at Grandpa, saying, "At that, they

97

seem not to know much about making money. Maybe they could use some of my ideas."

"Glory be!" chuckled Grandpa. "Let's hope they can resist the temptation."

Mom began clearing the table. "By the way, Tim, I laid something on your chest of drawers that I found in your jeans before I put them in the washer this morning. I wish you would remember to empty your pockets before you put clothes in the hamper."

Tim went to investigate. When he saw the flat, round piece which had figured in his dream about Old Hawk, Tim was amazed that he could have forgotten about that. "What a dope!" He sat down on his bed, turning the ornament around in his hand and remembering his vivid dream.

Marylu hadn't been the least impressed when he tried to tell her about that. She hadn't even asked to see the ornament. Probably her indifference had discouraged him from attaching much importance to this part of his find. But now he knew that Marylu was angry with him over their work in the shed. She might feel differently about Old Hawk, once she got over her mad.

"This might even be gold!" Tim thought. The stories about Old Hawk said that he had a secret cache of golden nuggets. The piece was dull-looking, but it could be tarnished gold.

Of course, Old Hawk himself had said the metal for the ornament had come from white men, and that his mother, descended from the Old Ones, had decorated it for him to wear around his neck. Well, then, maybe the markings told the secret of where Old Hawk's cache of gold nuggets was. Maybe Tim's cherished plan of owning a bicycle was about to be realized!

He thought of showing the piece to his father and asking his opinion. Most of the day tomorrow, Tim would be with Mrs. Sara, and she was more knowledgeable than anyone. Yes, he would show it to her. But he went to sleep that night without deciding whether or not he would tell her about his conversation with the dead Indian, and the things Old Hawk had told him.

14 BEGINNER'S LUCK

"Oh, Tim, you're just in time," Mrs. Sara said as Tim pushed through the door of the Research Center. "I have a million things to do, and today of all days we have visitors coming!"

"I thought Saturday was the open house," Tim said.

"Yes, but these folks from back East are passing through. They seemed so interested that we agreed to letting them have an early look."

"Yes, ma'am. Shall I start on my display now?" Plainly this was not a good time to ask her to look at Old Hawk's ornament, and maybe tell her about his dream, if dream it had been.

"Yes, do that; and also, I would like for you to watch for the visitors."

"Sure," Tim said. "I'll let you know the minute they come."

"Well, that won't be necessary. You see, I want you to act as guide for them."

"Me?" Tim exclaimed with astonishment.

"Everyone is so rushed today, trying to finish all the exhibits," Mrs. Sara explained. "And then we have been doing some special research which must be assembled and in the mail by evening. There's no one free to entertain our guests, unless you will."

"I've never done anything like this before," Tim said.

"I know it's a lot to ask of you. But it's the only way I'll be able to manage."

"I don't mind trying. I just hope I don't let you down," Tim said.

"In view of the remarkable finds you've made, you must have a big storehouse of beginner's luck which ought to carry you through this with no trouble. I hate sending those people away without answering their questions. So few Easterners know anything about the interesting and fascinating aspects of the Southwest . . . the Indians and the way they lived and all the myths and stories and folklore concerning them."

She hurried back to her piled-up desk, leaving Tim to transfer his finds from the small show case to a larger one.

"Boy," Tim thought to himself, "wait 'til Marylu and Mom and Dad and everybody hear about me being a guide at the Research Center!" He felt proud, but he was also alarmed. What would he say to those people when they came?

For quite a while, he worked on polishing the

glass of his show case. He had arranged his finds on its shelves and had just added the finishing touch of the sign Marylu had made, when he heard voices and footsteps.

A couple came in and introduced themselves as Mr. and Mrs. Bradford from New York City. They were middle-aged and pleasant looking.

Tim showed them everything and told them what he knew, as minutes ticked by and stretched into hours. He thought the day had gone rather well, but then at the end, the Bradfords insisted on seeing Mrs. Sara. He could only think that as a guide, he had flopped.

"Yes, Tim, what is it?" she asked, when he opened her door a crack and looked in.

Tim squeezed through. "I'm sorry to bother you," he said. "I've showed them everything, and I thought I answered all their questions okay. But the more I try to steer them away from bothering you, the more determined they are to see you. I'm sorry. I guess I'm not much good as a guide."

"Well, show them in, Tim. I'm sure it's not that," she said.

Mrs. Sara extended her hand to the Bradfords. "It's certainly a pleasure to have you here," she said.

"And it has been a real pleasure for us," Mr. Bradford said. "We have spent a good deal of time

102

visiting places of interest on this trip of ours, but never have we been more warmly received."

Mrs. Sara raised her eyebrows. "Really?"

"Indeed!" Mrs. Bradford chimed in. "This young man has told us the most amazing things."

Tim wondered if he could be hearing correctly. Without knowing he was doing it, he wiggled his ears. His Mom would have known from this that he was delighted past expression.

"I had never realized how clever the Indians were," Mrs. Bradford said. "They even knew how to make soap from the root of a plant."

"The yucca," her husband said. "Now wouldn't you think the soap manufacturers would want to know?"

Mrs. Sara answered him, "Some Indians in this area still use yucca root to make soap. I will admit that Tim's knowledge of this comes as a surprise to me."

If Tim said, "Old Hawk told me about that," she would be sure to question him. He decided to say nothing until the New Yorkers were gone. But wasn't this proof that his encounter with Old Hawk had been real? Tim's heart began to beat hard.

Mrs. Sara was saying to the Bradfords, "Yes, Tim has quite a knack for making finds. Didn't he show you his display of a big pot glued together, and a bowl with a bird design, and some other pieces from the Salado culture?"

Mr. Bradford laughed. "He told us those had been brought in by an amateur, but he didn't say who the amateur was. I should say he has a knack for finding relics! Have you some magic formula?" he asked Tim.

Old Hawk had said that Tim had a good eye, "like Indian." Nothing was magical about that, but the sharpest sight couldn't have informed him that Indians had made soap of yucca root. Although Tim felt warmly toward the Bradfords, he wished they would hurry and go, so he could tell Mrs. Sara all that had happened during the long night on the ledge.

15 THE ORNAMENT

THE VISITING Easterners were scarcely in their automobile before Tim had Old Hawk's ornament out of his pocket and into Mrs. Sara's hands. "Is it gold?" he asked hopefully.

"Gold! This? Oh, no, Tim! This is iron." She bent over it, her forehead wrinkling with concentration. "Where did you find it?"

"Near the cave where I found the other things."

"Curious . . . the symbols on it were copied from the Ancient Ones, but anything of iron is of quite recent date, of course. And then who could have left it near the cave, without disturbing the relics you found?"

"Maybe it was Old Hawk," Tim suggested.

She laughed and said, "Well, there have been tales and legends enough about him to suggest that he might have been everywhere and done everything. But why did you especially think of him?"

Looking at his feet, Tim forced himself to tell

her. "He used to wear that around his neck. His mother made it for him. She was descended from the Ancient Ones. I guess that's how she knew about their symbols."

Looking at him curiously, Mrs. Sara said in a quiet voice, "You're being very mysterious, Tim. And what makes you think you know that Old Hawk once wore this?"

"He told me so," Tim said.

For a while, neither of them said anything. She kept turning the ornament over in her hand, and finally she said, "The bird is very like the one on your bowl. Probably the association is with 'being free' rather than 'flight.' The sun and rain markings could have been an expression of the importance of Nature to the Indian; the things he learned from Nature, and his dependence on it to live."

Again they were silent, then she said, "What else did Old Hawk tell you?"

"About the yucca plant," Tim said, rubbing the floor hard with his toe.

"Do you want to tell me about that?"

"Yes'um, I do." As closely as he could remember it, he repeated their conversation.

Looking very thoughtful, Mrs. Sara said, "The Apache learned about iron from the white man. Never before had the Indian been able to fashion efficient tools. Iron was as valuable to him as gold was to the white man. It is too bad that we have always tended to value gold above wisdom. I wonder if that's what Old Hawk meant when he spoke of us as having 'a bad head.' " Sighing, she added, "Oh, Tim, your imagination is catching."

She handed the piece back to him. "This is valueless in itself and yet it does say such a lot to us, doesn't it? The Nature wisdom of the Old Ones is stamped here on the white man's iron. All my life, I've heard stories about Old Hawk's gold. Maybe his real treasure was this understanding that the good things of the Indians combined with good things of ours could add up to the good of us all."

Tim thought if that were so, Old Hawk's gold was scarcely the kind to buy him a bicycle. And yet he wasn't disappointed. This talk with Mrs. Sara was about the most exciting thing that had ever happened to him.

"Do you think you might like to become an archaeologist, Tim?" Mrs. Sara asked.

"Yes," he said. "I think I would."

"A good archaeologist is well trained, and very patient and thorough," Mrs. Sara said. "A truly great one has those qualities and something else that I hardly know how to describe—a power of feeling for things of the past and a talent for understanding what he finds as well as a talent just for finding. You would seem to have both. If you're serious about this, you ought to plan on assembling some of the equipment you will need—trowels and brushes to start with, and when you can afford it, a camera."

"A camera? Why?"

"So you can take pictures of artifacts in their original position and of the various locations. A camera is very nearly the most important tool an archaeologist has. Fifty dollars would get you an adequate one."

"Fat chance," Tim thought. One thing the summer had taught him was how hard it was on a ranch for a boy to earn money.

"You haven't said if you believe that I really talked with Old Hawk," Tim said.

"I don't disbelieve you, if that helps."

"Marylu just shrugged it off. She said I was dreaming."

"Perhaps you were dreaming. Didn't you tell me you went to sleep with the ornament in your hand?" Tim nodded.

"Use our big library dictionary over there, and look up the word 'psychometry,' " Mrs. Sara suggested. "Then come back and tell me what you think." She spelled the word for him.

He had trouble locating the word because he had forgotten the 'p,' which wasn't pronounced. He recalled his error by himself and finally found the right place.

> psy-chom-e-try, [*psych + metry*] 1. divination of facts concerning an object or its owner through contact with or proximity to the object.

Mrs. Sara was working on papers when he came back to her desk. She looked up and Tim asked, "What does 'divination' mean?"

"That's in the dictionary too," she answered, smiling at him.

Loyally, he plodded back to look up the new word. She followed him and read over his shoulder. "Oh, dear! You must think I plan to keep you here all day, looking up words. Quite simply, Tim, when you went to sleep ignorant of the fact that yucca roots were used to make soap, and woke up knowing, that would seem to have been divination whether or not it was through a dream."

"Wow!" Tim said. "Say, that's neat!"

Tim was quiet and thoughtful on the drive to pick up Marylu. He had questioned Mrs. Sara closely without persuading her to say more about "psychometry" and "divination." She seemed a little sorry that she had said as much as she had.

"You see, Tim, those of us who are under the scientific discipline tend to back away from what cannot be seen or weighed or proven. Shakespeare wrote that stranger things are on earth and in heaven than men have dreamed of, and perhaps he was right. Just the same, and for myself, I prefer the known paths." Then they had talked of other things.

109

Tim's Mom began to wonder about his quietness. "Did something unpleasant happen at the Center?" she asked.

"Oh, no, everything was fine," he said. "I moved my display, and I even got to be a guide to some visitors from back East."

"A guide! Why, Tim, you should be bursting at the seams. How did you know what to do?"

"They decided to stay another day so they could see some of the things I told them about," he said.

"Is that so?" Mom gave him a look of pride. "But doesn't it make you feel good to know you are important enough to the Center to be allowed to help in this way?"

"Oh, sure," said Tim. "I feel fine about that. It's just that, well, I've been given a lot to think about."

Mom lifted her eyebrows but said no more.

When they arrived at Jane's house, Marylu was watching for them from the door. She waved good-bye to Jane and ran to the car. Her cheeks were glowing and her eyes sparkled with happiness at seeing them.

She slipped her traveling case into the car and crawled in beside Tim. All her grumpy feelings toward him seemed to have vanished during her over-night stay. He was glad; he had missed her companionship.

"Why, Tim, you aren't your usual bubbling self.

Cheer up, I'm back, and all your troubles are here again," Marylu said teasingly.

Tim grinned and said, "Yeah," then lapsed into silence.

Mom turned onto the highway to the ranch. "I can't understand it, Marylu. He has been at the Research Center all day working on his display. And he even acted as a guide for some folks. He ought to be making us all miserable with his importance."

"Goodness, Tim, you're really getting to be right at home there," said Marylu.

"Yep." Tim looked at his hands. "Mrs. Sara said I could come as often as I wanted, to help and to learn about the things they do. I think she means it. It's a real break. I like it there." Tim grew silent again while Marylu chatted to Mom about her visit.

When they were home, Marylu headed for the horse corral. Tim followed her. She commenced to work on her mare with brush and curry comb. Tim swung himself up on the corral fence and watched, chewing his lip. It came hard to him to apologize to a girl.

Finally he said, "I'm sorry about those signs. I really didn't mean to trick you. I just got riled up. I really am sorry."

Marylu lowered her head and blinked back tears. She had a pretty fair idea of what this had cost him. Finally she said, "I'm sorry, too. While I was at Jane's, I got to thinking I haven't taken you seriously

111

enough about wanting a bike. It just sounded crazy to me."

"Yeah," he agreed. "I'm beginning to think it's crazy to want anything unless everybody else thinks you should want it."

She picked up one of Blue Girl's hind feet and began digging out pebbles and mud with a hoof pick. "No, you're entitled to want what you want. After all, the world would be an awful mess if everyone wanted exactly the same things. That's what I was thinking about at Jane's—that you never would have done that about those signs if you hadn't wanted a bike so much. You've tried all summer to earn the money, and everything has backfired on you, and instead of helping, I just got mad. So I'm sorry too, like I said."

"That's all right," he said gruffly. Trying to comfort her as well as himself, he added, "If I go on saving out of my allowance and what money-presents I get at Christmas and on my birthday, I ought to have enough in about two years."

This struck her as sad, because privately, she wondered if he wouldn't have outgrown his desire for a bike before then. She released Blue Girl's hoof, straightened, and said firmly, "There's just got to be a way, and tomorrow, we'll think of it. Let's take Sky and Blue Girl and start early, and have a nice picnic somewhere. Will you go if I pack a good lunch?"

"Sure," Tim said agreeably. "Sure, I'd like that. Only I don't think we're going to figure out any way to get me that bike."

He seemed to have given up hope. That just didn't sound like Tim. "We have to find a way, we just have to," Marylu thought.

16 OLD HAWK'S GOLD

IT RAINED during the night, and the next morning, when the sun's rays danced down through the juniper trees to the flat, the air was fresh and clear. This was a perfect day for a picnic, even in the summertime and in such a dry land. There was a nice breeze, and big thunderheads passing overhead made giant lakes of shade below.

It was still very early when Marylu shook Tim.

"Come on, get up! It's a wonderful day! I have cereal fixed for us, and the picnic lunch is almost ready."

She disappeared into the kitchen. Tim untangled himself from his sheet and swung his legs to the floor. He yawned and stretched and rubbed his head. He wondered why they were getting up so early to go on a picnic. Joe, on the foot of Tim's bed, peeked from one eye, then closed it. He couldn't even be tempted with lizards at this time of day.

"Come on, Tim," Marylu called again, softly to keep from waking anyone.

Tim dressed reluctantly, and before long they had the horses saddled and were on their way with the picnic lunch.

"Let's follow along the creek," suggested Marylu. "We ought to find a nice spot under a tree, and there's almost enough water to wade in after the rain."

They headed downstream, crossing under the highway through a big culvert, then winding back and forth with the stream.

Many small creatures had come to the creek for their morning water. They scurried away into the brush and rocks as the horses came near. Two cottontails flashed their white fluffs and scampered off. A jack rabbit hoisted his tall ears to judge what the commotion was about, before he leaped away across the rocks. Making soft whistles, two large quail ran and flew into some bushes to the left, attracting attention to themselves while their young ones scattered to cover on the right. And finally, as the riders rounded a bend, they came face to face with a brown-eyed doe and her fawn. The pretty creatures dashed away downstream, disappearing finally in a draw between rocky hills.

Marylu and Tim rode for an hour or two. The sun rose higher, and no more animals were seen at the stream edge. Marylu scanned the tree tops ahead.

"Look, Tim, there's a big willow farther on," she said.

They jogged along until they reached the place. The creek, in making a turn, had left a sand bar beneath the willow tree, and grass for the horses covered the bank alongside. Just downstream was a shallow pool.

"Oh, this is perfect for our picnic," Marylu said. She unsaddled Blue Girl and exchanged her bridle for a halter with a lead rope. She placed the saddle in the dry sand and hung the canteen on a tree branch.

"Come on down, Tim, and unsaddle Sky so they can enjoy the picnic too," Marylu said. She sat in the sand, leaning against her saddle.

Blue Girl had edged to the pool of water. The mare sucked in mouthfuls. Then she stepped into the water, cautiously pawing to reassure herself of the safety of the sand beneath. Suddenly, she lay down and rolled over.

Tim unsaddled Sky. "Man, what a clown!" he said about Blue Girl as she rolled back and forth, splashing.

Marylu laughed. She pulled off her boots and socks and rolled up her jeans. "I'm next!"

Marylu pulled on Blue Girl's rope. The mare got up and shook the water from her coat, while Marylu waded into the stream, curling her toes into the sand as she went.

"Oh, this feels good!" She paraded up and down while Tim put a rope halter on Sky. Finally Marylu sloshed out of the water and got a carrot out of the picnic sack.

"Watch this, Tim," she said. She let Blue Girl smell of the carrot.

"Now," she said, addressing Blue Girl, "let's hear you count. Count to three," she ordered. "Come on, now, here we go . . . ONE!" As Marylu raised her arm high and lowered it, Blue Girl raised her head and lowered it. "TWO!" counted Marylu, raising her arm as Blue Girl repeated her head movement. "And . . . THREE!" Blue Girl nodded her head into a low bow again; and then raised it quickly to claim her reward of a carrot.

"Hey!" said Tim in amazement. "When did she learn to do that?" Blue Girl munched her carrot as she made her way to the grass beneath the willow tree.

"Oh, we've been working on it for a long time," Marylu said with pride. She got the lunch sack and began to spread their lunch on newspapers she had brought.

Settling himself against his saddle, Tim ate and watched Blue Girl grazing. The morning light came in a stream through a gap in the branches of the willow tree. As Blue Girl stepped into its slanting brightness, Tim could hardly believe his eyes. He was looking at a blue horse.

"Hey, look," he yelled. "She really is blue!"

"Sure she is," said Marylu. "I told you she was!"

"Wow!" Tim took a bite of sandwich and chewed

117

it thoughtfully. "I guess Blue G's a right good horse. At first, I . . . well, I didn't think she was so much," he confessed, "but she's really SOME horse, being that color, and learning tricks, and everything."

He cracked a hard boiled egg and began to peel it. "Do you suppose I could teach Sky to do that? It's funny, but when you have a horse around all the time, you don't think about doing things like that with him."

"I guess I had been day-dreaming for years about what I wanted to do with a horse when I got one," Marylu agreed. "You didn't have to day-dream about Sky; so you don't know about the kind of thing that pops into your head."

"Oh, don't I? You know the hill by the house that drops down to the creek?"

"Uh-huh," Marylu nodded.

"Well, how do you think it would be to go down that on a bike?" Tim asked.

"Oh, Tim, that would be wild!" she exclaimed, remembering the big steep hill. "Ooooh! That would be really fun."

"Or what about riding a bike with no hands . . . or maybe standing up on the cross bar after you got it going good," he added.

"Oh, Tim, I guess you have done your share of day-dreaming about the bike you want so much. In the night I thought up some new ideas. Do you want to hear about them?"

118

"Sure, go ahead." His lunch finished, he stretched out with his head against his saddle, to listen.

"Well, what if you chopped a whole lot of extra firewood? I'll bet your Dad would let you sell some to the other ranchers around here."

"They all have their own firewood, free for the chopping," said Tim.

"Oh," said Marylu. "Well, what about the cats? There are cats and kittens all over the barn. I heard your Dad say there were too many. Maybe he would let you sell a few. Some of them are very cute."

"When someone needs a cat, we just give it. We couldn't sell cats!"

Marylu sighed. "Well, how about growing vegetables? Radishes come up in a few days, and beets, and corn grows quickly too. Maybe you could plant cantaloupe and watermelons. Then later this summer, you could have a stand down by the highway."

It wouldn't work, Tim knew. In a few weeks, the water in the creek would go underground. "Then we'll have to save what water dribbles into the tank at the house for drinking and washing," he explained. "Dad builds tanks for the cattle so they'll have enough to get through 'til the rains come. But we never have water enough in summertime to grow extra things."

Tim skimmed a rock into the pool of water. "I know you're trying to help. Until the other day, probably I would have gotten all steamed up about those ideas."

119

Marylu looked at Tim. Yes, he certainly seemed different. "What happened the other day to change your mind?" she asked.

Tim brought Old Hawk's ornament out of his pocket. "This did, I guess."

"Oh, that thing you found at the cave. Didn't Mrs. Sara want it for the Center?"

"Naw, it's not good for anything. The really old Indians didn't use iron. I guess I'm the only one this means anything to."

"Because you found it, you mean."

"No, because Old Hawk gave it to me," Tim said firmly.

"Oh, Tim, do you still insist on believing that?"

"Mrs. Sara believes me," Tim said.

Marylu was astonished. "Oh, Tim, she couldn't!"

He told her about the big words in the dictionary, and some of the things Mrs. Sara had told him.

"Old Hawk said his mother made the markings. She was descended from the Old Ones, and she must have made them to show how the Old Ones felt about things. Don't you see, it was her gift to her son, so he would never forget their ancient secrets. Old Hawk gave it to me because he wanted me to know those secrets too."

Conscious again of the curious warmth of the ornament in his hand, Tim added, "Haven't you ever been someplace or had a feeling about something that you felt was, well, as if it belonged just to you?"

Marylu thought about how she had felt about the

120

red, rugged hills the day she and Tim rode out to set the coyote trap. She remembered the times she had sketched a string of wild horses along a lonely mesa top, or the times she had sat cold, but thrilled, on a stump, trying to capture a stormy sky with her water colors. Yes, she knew that feeling . . . about something that could belong to no one else. Perhaps it was a gift.

"I think I understand, Tim," she said. "It's a wonderful feeling to have. I think it's just about the most wonderful and important feeling anyone can have," she added.

There wasn't much left to discuss. They talked of other things, and they built two fine sand castles, then staged a pretend-battle until the castles fell down. Finally Marylu cleaned up the picnic things while Tim saddled the horses, and they started home.

After they had turned their horses into the corral, they collected their picnic gear and trudged into the house, where Mom, Grandpa Cone, and Dutch were together having coffee.

"My, you two got an early start this morning. How was the picnic?" asked Mom.

"Great!" Tim said, emptying the canteen.

"We found a neat spot." Marylu threw away the trash from their picnic, then washed the spoons.

"The mining men were here this morning,"

Dutch told his son. "They found out about your claim."

"Yeah? Well, I still don't think it's right for them to mess up the Indian ruins that way."

"As a matter of fact, they felt a little bad about that themselves. They have come up with a scheme they hope you will think is all right. They intend to be careful about where they do any digging or drilling. They also promised to sift through all the dirt they remove, and if they find anything, they will let you know immediately. Does that sound fair? You'd have all that hard digging done for you."

"Well, sure," Tim said. "Yeah, I'd like that fine."

"They were a little perplexed about your claim," Dutch told him. "In fact, it was the first time they had come up against anything like it. Finally they decided in order to keep everything entirely legal, they would just give you this." Dutch handed Tim an envelope.

"What is it?" Tim asked, opening the envelope.

"It's a lease for you to sign," Dutch said.

"And a check for fifty dollars!" He waved it exuberantly. "Is it mine? Is it mine for leasing them my claim?"

"Yep," said Dutch. "That's the deal."

Tim stared at the check. Marylu moved to look over his shoulder and see for herself.

"Oh, Tim," she said, shaking his arm, "you've got it. You've got your bike after all."

"Yeah," said Tim. "I just can't believe it."

"I know, I know," she said. "I can't believe it either. Oh, Tim, you can get just the bike you want. It's wonderful!"

Dutch rubbed his chin and pursed his lips. Mom beamed, and Grandpa Cone grinned with pleasure.

Marylu said suddenly, "Let me see that thing again." Tim handed her the check, but it turned out that what she wanted to examine was Old Hawk's ornament. "I'm beginning to believe he really did give this to you," she said, tracing the design with her forefinger. "It's spooky, kind-of, that nothing panned out that you did to get the bike. But when you filed the claim on Rose Hill, that was to save the Indian relics. You weren't thinking then about getting the bike. And now, you can!"

"Hey, how about that!" Tim marveled.

"Well, I suppose you'll want to go to town tomorrow and get that bike, first thing," Dutch said.

"Well, sir, I sure do want to go to town," Tim agreed. "But I don't want to buy a bike."

"You don't *what?*" asked Marylu.

"I don't want to buy a bike," Tim repeated. "I want to buy a camera."

"A camera?" Marylu wondered if she had heard correctly. "You mean a 'click, click' camera?"

"Uh-huh," said Tim. "It's a real handy piece of equipment for an archaeologist to have."

"Good grief! And they talk about women changing their minds!"

"Time changes many things," reflected Grandpa Cone.

"I guess it takes a little sifting to find what you're really looking for." Tim had taken back the ornament from Marylu. He felt its familiar warmth in his hand. He went out the front door carrying Old Hawk's gifts, the ornament and the check.

A little breeze rustling through the trumpet vine sounded almost like chuckling. Distinctly, he heard the words, "Now you have good head, too!" No one was near, of course.

He walked across the yard as Marylu popped out the front door and followed him. "Are you sure you won't be sorry, Tim?" she asked.

"A little bit," he admitted. "It would have been fun for a while. But even you don't care about your bike much anymore. I would have gotten tired of it."

"I know you would have," agreed Marylu.

"And think what I can do with a camera. I can take pictures of all the sites I know about and all the things I find and . . . "

"Oh, yes, Tim. And we could have it along on rides and take pictures of things, like the deer we saw this morning and the quail."

"Hey, we sure could."

"And you know, Tim," continued Marylu, "I could bring my bike up here anytime, and we could try it out the way you wanted to do."

Tim grinned, "Yeah, that's a great idea. You know, for a girl you do some real good thinking!"

124